BLOODLINE

They were a mixed bunch aboard the noon stage for Lateness: the enigmatic widow, Leonora Grey; the young drifter, Cal Heeney, and the mysterious Mr Smith. Why was Sheriff Lou Benson trailing the stage, and why was he so concerned that Mrs Grey was leaving town? Any stage coach ride runs the risk of attack, but this one seemed particularly doomed. Would the passengers cope with events and the new menace of Ord Whittaker and his gang of gunslingers on the *Bloodline?*

BLOODLINE

BLOODLINE

by

Dan Claymaker

Dales Large Print Books
Long Preston, North Yorkshire,
England.

British Library Cataloguing in Publication Data.

Claymaker, Dan
    Bloodline.

    A catalogue record for this book is
    available from the British Library

    ISBN 1-85389-699-3 pbk

First published in Great Britain by Robert Hale Ltd., 1994

Copyright © 1994 by Dan Claymaker

The right of Dan Claymaker to be identified as the author
of this work has been asserted by him in accordance with
the Copyright, Designs and Patents Act, 1988

Published in Large Print January, 1997 by arrangement with
Robert Hale Ltd.

Dales Large Print is an imprint of
Library Magna Books Ltd.
Printed and bound in Great Britain by
T.J. International Ltd., Cornwall, PL28 8RW.

For G.S.,
always a bold traveller

ONE

The noon stage set to make the three-day haul from Steeple to Lateness was already drawn up at the stage office when Leonora Grey, still pale and tired-eyed following the funeral of her husband, checked in for the journey with just one small valise.

'Sure am sorry t' see yuh leavin' like this, ma'am,' said Fletch Jones, the stage clerk, hurrying from behind the counter. 'Don't seem right somehow. Shouldn't be so. Mister Grey dyin' like that and no critter brought t' book f' it. T'ain't justice. Why would anyone wanna do a thing like that, eh? Why—and in cold blood too. Nossir, t'ain't justice.' He eyed the small valise. 'That all yuh luggage, ma'am?'

'That's all,' said the woman.

Fletch scratched the top of his head. 'Travellin' a mite light, ain't yuh? That mean yuh mebbe comin' back?'

'No, Mister Jones, I shall not be coming back.'

'Well, I guess yuh know best.' Fletch picked up the valise and walked to the office door. 'Stage leaves in five minutes, ma'am. First stop High Rivers this evenin'. Shake Reams is drivin', Bill Soames ridin' alongside him. Yuh can rely on them. Good men. Yuh got two passengers f' company.' He paused, smiling thinly. 'Two fellas—but I figure they're gentlemen. One's already aboard. The other's—' He peered from the doorway along the boardwalk. 'On his way now.'

'Thank you, Mister Jones, you have been most helpful,' said the woman.

'No trouble at all, ma'am, no trouble. Like I say, just sorry t' see yuh goin'. Town won't seem the same without yuh. And that's a fact. But don't yuh fret, ma'am, whoever it was that shot yuh husband like that—and in the back too—ain't goin' t' get away with it. We'll get him. Yessir! He'll hang high here in Steeple one day, yuh can bank on it.'

'I'm sure I can,' smiled the woman.

10

'And thank you again.'

Fletch Jones nodded and grunted and carried Leonora Grey's valise to the stage.

Shake Reams cracked the team into life and rolled the stage for Lateness out of Steeple at two minutes past noon. He had three passengers aboard: the widow Grey; a young, broad-shouldered, smiling fellow by the name of Cal Heeney, and an older, soberly dressed, quiet spoken gent who had checked in as Mr Smith.

At seven minutes past noon, Sheriff Lou Benson stood in the stage office and watched in silence as Fletch Jones flicked through his records.

'Don't reckon there's a deal more I can tell yuh, Lou,' he said, adjusting his spectacles as he pored over the words and figures. 'Mrs Grey yuh know about. The young fella, Heeney—well, he talked plenty about nothin', never stopped smilin', paid straight up f' his passage and climbed aboard. No luggage. Mr Smith—he hardly said a word, savin' t' be polite. Like Heeney, he paid through

11

t' Lateness. No luggage. Never set eyes on either of them before. Must've drifted int' town yesterday.'

'Both the men armed?' asked Benson.

'Sidearms. Colts. Nothin' more.'

Benson grunted. 'How was Mrs Grey?'

'Sorta quiet. Never said a deal. Looked tired, but smart as ever. Travellin' awful light, if yuh ask me. Still... Heck, she's a beauty and no mistake! Sam Grey sure roped himself a charmer there—and him bein' all them years older than her. Just goes t' show...soft sand drifts t' old rock easy as it does t' new stone.' Fletch coughed lightly. 'No disrespect intended, o'course. Beats me, though, how and why Sam came t' die like that. Just don't make no sense at all.'

Benson grunted again. 'Okay, Fletch, thanks a lot.' His eyes narrowed. 'Now here's what I want yuh t' do...'

It was ten minutes past one-o'clock when Sheriff Lou Benson left Steeple alone and rode out on the north-west trail heading for Lateness. His mount was packed for

12

a long ride, but Benson sat the horse easy and relaxed until he reached a turn on the trail three miles out of town where he veered away on a more northerly track that would take him across country to High Rivers.

Only then did he urge the roan mare to a faster pace.

TWO

'Well, now, seein' as how we got some hours before we reach High Rivers, seems t' me it might be sociable t' get t' know each other. Sorta pass the time. I'm Cal Heeney. Pleased t' meet yuh both.'

Heeney relaxed in the corner of the stage, and smiled. It was a smile that broke naturally on his tanned, handsome face, with its rock-like jaw, gleam of even teeth, shining blue eyes that gathered the light to them and mirrored a razored sense of humour.

13

'Leonora Grey,' said the woman, with no more than the flicker of a soft grin.

The older man turned his head to look at Heeney and murmured simply, 'Smith.'

'Well, Miss Grey—'

'Mrs,' corrected the woman.

'Pardon me, ma'am,' smiled Heeney. 'Wouldn't have figured yuh f' a married lady.' His blue eyes danced.

'I am widowed, Mister Heeney. Since last week.'

Smith's head turned again, this time to go back to watching the drift of passing scenery.

'Oh,' said Heeney. 'Now that's sad, ma'am, real sad. My apologies.'

'That's quite all right. You were not to know.'

Heeney slapped his hands on his knees. 'I'm goin' clear through t' Lateness. Never been this far West before. Nice country. Shade hot and dusty, but nice.' He paused. 'Yuh from these parts, Mrs Grey?'

'Back East until I married.'

'Took yuh f' an eastern lady, ma'am.

14

They gotta sorta special look—leastways, that's been my experience.'

Leonora Grey smiled demurely.

'And y'self, Mr Smith?' continued Heeney. 'Yuh from hereabouts?'

Smith's head turned slowly. 'No,' he said flatly.

'I'm all f' travellin',' Heeney went on lightly. 'Pays a man t' see as much of this country as he can, I reckon. In m' own case, that's a matter of driftin' through it, I guess.' His smile broadened. 'Here, there, just about anywheres. I make out. More luck than judgement mostly. But a man's gotta take what he can when it offers, and what's life for if it ain't f' livin'? That's me—livin' life, just as it comes.'

'And goes,' murmured Smith to the scenery.

Shake Reams held the team to a steady pace as the stage for Lateness rolled steadily north-west. This was always the easy part of the haul, he reckoned; flat, open country, a well worn trail with horses fresh enough to find their feet without straining. It gave

15

the driver time to think, watch for the upcoming shifts in the weather, safe in the knowledge that he would be pulling into the post at High Rivers a good half-hour before the sun sank from view.

Shake knew every twist and turn of the three-day trail, almost every rock and stone of it. 'Reckon I could take a team t' Lateness blindfold!' he had once claimed. But there was something about this trip that was already bothering him.

Maybe it was Leonora Grey.

Sure, he had known she would be leaving Steeple after the shooting of her husband. She had said so straight out, and sure, no one was blaming her. The shooting of Sam Grey had been a grisly, cowardly affair, a tragedy his widow would want to put well behind her. But it troubled Shake that Mrs Grey had so little luggage.

Same thing had troubled Fletch Jones. How come she was travelling light, he wondered, when he knew for a fact that Sam had lavished clothes, jewellery, perfumes on her like there would be no sun-up? Was she leaving all that wealth back at the ranch? Seemed unlike a woman by his reckoning. And what in tarnation was she planning to do in Lateness? Change stages, keep going, settle? Or maybe she was meeting somebody.

And then there was that fellow by the name of Smith.

Well, figured Shake, he may or may not be Mr Smith (he wished he had a dollar for every 'Smith' he had carted!) but this man's face sure was familiar. Somewhere, some time, he had seen 'Mister Smith' before. But where, and when, and how come he should be bothered by one particular face among the hundreds he had seen as passengers? And how come this Smith had turned up in Steeple, and what, he wondered, was the man's business in Lateness?

As for his other passenger, Cal Heeney, well, he was just a loud-talking, swaggering drifter with a big mouth and a bigger eye for the women, he would wager. Mrs Grey had best look out for that one, he reckoned. Widowhood would hardly rate

17

in Heeney's accounting.

But there was one other thing troubling Shake more than most on that day.

Less than an hour out of Steeple he had seen a lone rider moving West on the drift of the far northern hills. Nothing unusual about that—there were always riders heading West these days—but that was not the point. The point was there was no mistaking the shape of this rider; tall and straight but easy. He would know it anywhere.

Now why in hell, he pondered, was Sheriff Lou Benson riding West alone and, so it seemed, keeping the stage in his sights?

One thing about this job, sighed Shake to himself, you never got bored!

Leonora Grey had been watching Smith discreetly since Cal Heeney had finally run out of talk about himself and fallen asleep.

She had been trying to fathom just how old Smith was. Hard to tell, she thought. His face was worn and weathered, the hair at his temples a rich silvery hue, but his eyes had a sharpness and brightness about them that deceived. It was in them, she had decided, that you could see the measure of the man: shrewd, clever, calculating and deep thinking in his silence. And doubtless fast with that fancy Colt at his waist.

She smiled softly as he turned to face her.

'Sorry t' hear about yuh loss, Mrs Grey,' he said. 'Death don't stand easy, more so when it's close.'

She lowered her eyes. 'Thank you. Like you say, especially when it's close.' She paused a moment. 'You a married man, Mister Smith?'

'No, ma'am, never had that pleasure. Never had the time, I guess. Always been alone.'

'People should not be alone.'

'Mebbe so—but you are, right now, and travellin' at that. That a wise thing f' a woman to be doin' without a companion?'

'Depends on the woman, surely.'

Smith grunted. 'A careful observation.

19

Yuh sound as if yuh done a fair bit.'

'My share. Stages are stages anywhere. Passengers passing company. You a traveller?'

The man's stare hardened. 'Some,' he said.

'Back East?'

'Never East.'

Leonora Grey smiled again. 'Then I must be mistaken. Your face looks familiar. I thought we might have met before I married my husband back East. Some years ago, of course.'

Smith grunted again. 'How did yuh husband die, ma'am, or shouldn't I ask?'

'He was shot, Mister Smith—in the back,' said the woman without hesitation. 'Murdered.'

'Know who did it?'

'No, not yet. My husband was a considerable landowner. He had a wide circle of associates.'

'And at least one enemy,' observed Smith, turning his gaze back to the scenery.

Leonora Grey sat in silence, listening

20

to the steady roll of wheels, the creak of wood and leather and the crack of Shake Reams' whip.

Lou Benson reined his mount to a halt at the foot of the ridge and shielded his eyes against the sun's glare as he scanned the sweep of the main northern trail. His diversion through the hill country had put him a half-hour ahead of the stage. Good, he thought; at this rate he would be settled short of High Rivers well ahead of its arrival. Just as he had planned.

He was sure now that Shake Reams had spotted him. That too was as he planned. He reached for his waterflask and sated his thirst. The heat of the afternoon was fierce; there was no breeze, nothing save sand and rock and clear blue sky. He would be glad when this trip was over, when he had Sam Grey's killer safely under lock and key in Lateness.

His eyes narrowed on a distant swirl of dust. Stage was coming, right on time. He urged the mare to a canter and rode on.

THREE

The staging post at High Rivers was a long, squat, Southfacing building with a veranda running the length of its sun-drenched frontage. It provided accommodation for overnight passengers heading West and for its boss, Big John Morton, who had been running the post for almost a decade.

It was an isolated place, ten miles to the East of the twisting River Toomey, set square in an endless spread of dry-rock and desert country, and a lonely existence for Big John whose only company was the spare horses and the passengers he met and fed when the stage rolled in. He looked forward particularly to the arrival of Shake Reams on the Lateness run, for with Shake came Big John's supply of whisky and baccy. And that was a day to be reckoned!

But on this day, an hour before Shake

was due, the reckoning was of a different order.

The accommodation had been ransacked and pillaged, the horses turned loose, and most of the fresh water supply spilled over the searing sand. Big John Morton lay stiff and dead in a pool of blood on the veranda, shot twice through the head at close range.

The only living things that afternoon at the post were the flies, and the only sounds the unceasing buzz of them. All the rest was death and destruction.

'Twenty minutes, I reckon,' called Shake to his stage partner, Bill Soames. 'Made good time.'

Soames nodded and grinned.

'Big John'll have the steaks in the pan!' added Shake with a slap of his lips as he urged the team to a faster pace. Once clear of the knoll at the ridge and they would be there...

Shake knew there was something wrong within seconds of rounding the knoll. There was no smoke at the post for one thing, no cooking underway. Big John was never late with his steaks and coffee. There were no horses in the corral, and why in tarnation were those water butts strewn over the front of the place like the leftovers of some bar brawl? What the heck was Big John thinking of? And where was he? He was always there when the stage cleared the knoll.

'Sonofabitch,' called Shake to Bill Soames, pointing ahead. 'Now what in hell d' yuh make of that?'

Soames peered, shrugged and eased his Winchester across his knees.

Another quarter-mile and Shake was absolutely certain something was wrong.

He began to slow the team, ease away their sweating pace, then finally brought them and the stage to a halt, the horses steaming in the swirls of dust. He peered closer as the dust cleared, but, as if instinctively aware of trouble, did not call out. He simply looked at Bill Soames, waited a moment and then climbed carefully down from the stage, his gaze moving slowly over the scattered mess.

All he could hear was the terrible silence and all around him, it seemed, the buzz of flies.

He was walking towards the post, his steps ponderous, his gaze bewildered, when Smith joined him.

'There,' said the man. 'On the veranda.'

'Hell!' murmured Shake as he stared at the fly-blackened body of Big John Morton.

A sharp stone in the shoe of the mare's right hoof had delayed Lou Benson's arrival at the ridge rock cover just short of High Rivers by twenty minutes. Shake would have the stage drawn up at the post by now, he reckoned, as he reined the mount to a halt in a drift of creek flanking the trail.

He had been set to take another look at the mare's hoof when a still smouldering patch of ash from a recent camp fire caught his eye. He hitched the mount and wandered over to the wispy curls of smoke.

More than half-a-dozen men and mounts, he reckoned, judging by the prints in the sandy surrounds. Here overnight and not many hours gone. He rubbed his chin thoughtfully. Drifters, he wondered? Cattlemen moving West in search of work? Or maybe...

His eyes narrowed as they settled on a discarded waterflask lodged between rocks in a sprawl of brush. He crossed to it, picked it up and ran his fingers over the worn leather, the broken strap. The flask had at some time been shot through. Useless for holding water, but it was not the scorched bullet holes that held his attention. He was more interested in the initials scratched on the side of the flask.

'O.W.,' he murmured. 'O.W...'

Benson felt the sudden chill of cold sweat in his neck. 'Ord Whittaker,' he murmured again. Could it be—the Whittaker gang this far West? Last he heard of them they had been 'way South in Louisiana, but that had been months back. No knowing what havoc and mayhem they had been creating since, saving that it would be havoc and definitely mayhem, with looting, raping and killing thrown in for good measure.

The Whittaker gang, he mused. There was a high price on Ord's head, dead or alive. But what were the gang doing here? Riding hard from trouble, or riding hard to find it? Either way, trouble rode with the Whittaker mob.

He threw the flask aside and walked back to his mount. Change of plan, he figured. He mounted up, turned the mare and rode out of the ridge cover to the open trail heading for High Rivers.

'Well,' said Cal Heeney, pacing the veranda of the staging post impatiently, 'so what do we do now? Stand about?' There was a gleam of sweat on his brow as his gaze moved over the faces of Leonora Grey, Smith and Shake Reams.

'Nossir, we do not!' said Shake. 'First thing we do is get this place cleared up. Then we see if there's any water left and get ourselves somethin' t' eat. Bill and me'll take care of the horses.' He turned to Leonora Grey. 'Be obliged if I could leave yuh t' sort out the food side, ma'am.'

27

'Yuh mean we stayin' here?' snapped Heeney.

'Don't have no choice, mister. We got no spare horses, and the team that got us here ain't goin' no place till sunup.'

'He's right,' said Smith quietly. 'We can't move till mornin'.'

'And then what, Mister Reams?' asked the woman.

'Then we think again, ma'am.'

'Who the hell would've done this, and why?' said Heeney.

'Don't know on both counts, and that's the truth of it,' answered Shake. 'But whoever it was is sure goin' t' pay f' it with their necks, I can promise yuh that! I known Big John all m' life. One of the nicest fellas around. Wouldn't have harmed a hair on yuh head. Not a darned hair...' Shake's voice drifted away.

'We need t' get news of this t' the Sheriff back at Steeple,' said Smith.

Leonora Grey glanced quickly at him. 'When?'

'Soon as we can come first light.'

'And how we goin' t' do that?' asked Heeney.

'No need t' worry,' said Shake. 'He's comin' t' us, right now.'

They turned to see Lou Benson riding in through the last of the pale evening light.

FOUR

The night at High Rivers gathered black as crows, velvet smooth and silent under a soft yellow moon and a scattering of stars. The shadows were deep and the glow of the lamp in the staging post like a touch of flame in the stillness. The only sound in that empty land was the drone of Lou Benson's voice.

'I gotta tell yuh straight that I ain't in any doubt about who killed Big John, not after what I found back there at the ridge. The Whittaker gang rode in here some time this afternoon. Mebbe they were in need of food and water; mebbe lookin' f' liquor; mebbe all three. Big John wouldn't have stood a chance. Ord Whittaker don't leave any livin' in his wake.'

'Who are the Whittaker gang, anyhow?' asked Heeney, draining his mug of coffee.

'I heard of them,' said Smith. 'A mean bunch of roughriders and gunslingers. Worked the territories t' the South more often than not—robbin', killin', takin' what took their fancy, women included. They all come the same t' Ord. Yuh don't tangle with him lest yuh forced.'

'S'right,' said Shake. 'But I ain't known him trail his boys this far West before.'

'Yuh tangled with this character, Mister Smith?' asked Benson carefully.

Smith's grey eyes were unblinking. 'I only heard of him.'

Benson grunted. 'Don't make a deal of odds one way or the other. Fact is the Whittaker gang's in the territory, and that's bad news.'

'And the other fact, Sheriff, is that we are here,' said Heeney. 'Yuh got any plan in mind?'

'We are going on, aren't we, Mister

Benson?' asked Leonora Grey anxiously. 'I mean, you're not thinking, are you—'

'This stage will leave on the next leg of the journey t' Lateness come sun-up,' said Benson, catching the woman's faint sigh of relief. 'There's a day's run from here t' Makeshift. We're goin' t' make that run. Bill Soames'll take m' mount and ride back t' Steeple. I want some men out here, and I want a wire sent through t' the Territorial Marshal. I'll take Bill's place alongside Shake.'

'Lucky f' us yuh were out this way, Sheriff,' said Smith, lighting a cigar. 'Pure coincidence, I suppose?'

'Sheriff often rides out this way, don't yuh, Sheriff?' said Shake hurriedly.

Benson finished his coffee. 'Often,' he replied.

Smith nodded. 'Well, I'm sure we're all grateful t' yuh.' He blew a slow drift of smoke.

'But won't it be dangerous, Sheriff?' said Leonora Grey. 'I mean, if the Whittaker gang are still around and they know we've been here, won't they—'

'Yuh, can leave that t' Lou here, ma'am,' grinned Shake. 'Lou and me'll see yuh safe t' Lateness, yuh can bet on that. Ain't that so, Lou?'

Benson smiled.' We'll do our best, Mrs Grey.'

Heeney and Smith settled their stares on him, but said nothing.

Later, when the others were preparing to bed themselves down for the night, Lou Benson and Shake Reams stood alone together on the post's veranda and watched the darkness deepening. There was a look of concern on Shake's face as he turned to the sheriff.

'Mrs Grey's right, yuh know,' he said. 'With the Whittaker gang still around we could be headin' straight int' real trouble. They might even decide t' wait f' us on the trail t' Makeshift. Heck, that's wide open country, Lou, and with a woman aboard—'

'We ain't takin' the trail t' Makeshift,' said Benson.

Shake frowned. 'We ain't?'

'That's just what Ord Whittaker would expect us t' do. He'll have figured there's a stage due outta here sometime, and we'd be easy pickin's anywhere between High Rivers and Makeshift. So we don't take that trail. We'll head North, cross the Toomey and make f' Cascade Pass.'

'Cascade Pass!' spluttered Shake. 'But that's one helluva place, Lou. Real rough. It'll add a day t' the journey, and I ain't sure as how I can get this outfit through country like that.'

'Yuh'll do it,' said Benson. 'Yuh goin' t' have to. It's either that, or turn back t' Steeple, and that's somethin' I don't wanna do.'

'Yuh got some good reason? That why yuh out here?'

'I got a reason,' said Benson.

Shake sighed. 'Reckoned so. I spotted yuh trailin' us miles back there, and I ain't known yuh come this way in months.'

Benson stared into the night. 'My reason, Shake, is t' bring Sam Grey's killer t' book.'

'But how come—'

'Not now, Shake. I'll explain later when we're clear of the Whittaker boys.'

Shake lifted his hat and scratched the top of his head. 'Beats me. Still, guess yuh know what yuh doin'. But I'll tell yuh somethin', Lou, this sure is a strange bunch I'm shippin' t' Lateness. I don't figure either of them fellas. Who the heck are they? Where they come from? And there's somethin' about Mrs Grey I don't fathom. Where's her luggage? If she's pullin' outta Steeple f' good, how come she ain't carryin' more? She leavin' all them clothes and jewellery Sam bought f' her behind? T'ain't like any woman of my reckonin', but if she is—'

Lou Benson laid a hand on Shake's shoulder. 'Let's make it an early night, shall we? I want Bill Soames saddled up and away t' Steeple at sun-up, and we gotta big day ahead of us.'

'Yuh can say that again!' sighed Shake.

Leonora Grey could not sleep. She lay on the bed in the small room and stared into the patch of bright moonlight on the wall facing her. There was a face in it, a face she was sure she knew, conjured perhaps from somewhere deep in her subconscious, that watched her like a haunting. Its expression did not change; the eyes did not blink, the lips did not move. It grew clearer in the glow, faded, grew again, as if beckoning, willing her to stare, to recognise. Or was it all imagination, she wondered, a trick of the light, the shift of some playful shadow?

She wished she could remember, summon some fragment of the past that would give the face a name, a place, its part in her life. But there was nothing. Only the shape in the patch of light.

She closed her eyes and thought of the events of the day, of what tomorrow might bring, of all that had led up to this journey to Lateness, and then of Sam Grey there, once again, dead on the floor of the rambling old ranch at Steeple...

She heard the creak of the floorboard at her back, but did not move. She felt no fear, made no sound. She had only to wait. Another creak, the closeness of an unseen presence, and then the touch of the hand that slid slowly over her shoulder, laid aside the tress of hair in her neck, slid on, down, down...until the warmth of the hand held her breast, and stayed.

She sighed. The patch of moonlight was suddenly empty.

FIVE

'No town's Boot Hill grave f' Big John Morton! And that's f' sure! His life had been here, and here's where he's goin' t' stay!' Shake Reams had insisted at the first fingering of dawn light. And so he and Lou Benson had buried the man at the staging post in full view of the trail he had watched and worried over for the better part of his life. The simple inscription on the rough wooden cross read: Big John. Stage Man.

Two hours later, Bill Soames had saddled up and headed back to Steeple, the stage had been drawn ready, the team hitched and the run for Cascade Pass got underway.

'We should hit the river well before noon,' called Shake, rolling the stage on its sand and rock route northwards. 'I'll need t' rest the team there and find fresh water. The Toomey's fed from the mountain streams thereabouts, so we might be lucky.' He urged the team to a steady pace. 'Then there's Will and May Banks' homestead a mile or so before we reach the hard trail t' the Pass. Mebbe they'll help out with food.' He glanced at Lou Benson who held his silence in his long stare ahead. 'O' course,' Shake went on, 'we could've waited back at the post, and yuh could've sent Bill f' help f' us. We could be doin' most anythin', save scrawlin' over this Godforsaken territory... But I guess not.'

'Just drive 'em, Shake,' said Benson, his stare still fixed on the horizon. 'Just drive 'em...'

'Rough goin',' said Heeney, rolling in his corner-seat to a sudden lurch of the stage. His smile spread over his face like a sand streak splitting under sun glare. 'No place f' dozin', that's f' sure!' The smile softened and withered with the next lurch. 'Yuh sleep well, ma'am?' he asked. 'Such as yuh could in those bug-bounced beds!'

'Well enough, Mister Heeney,' said Leonora Grey with a gentle smile.

Heeney lurched to another roll. 'This travellin' West is sure turnin' out t' be some experience,' he grinned. 'Not that I mean that lightly, yuh understand,' he added hastily. 'Don't get me wrong. Real shame about the fella back there. Them Whittaker boys must be one helluva mean mob.'

'They are,' murmured Smith.

'We're lucky the sheriff happened along like that. Makes a difference, don't yuh reckon?'

'Mebbe,' said Smith.

'We seem to have left the main trail,' said Leonora Grey.

Smith grunted. 'We've turned North.'

'Is that a good thing, Mister Smith?'

'That all depends, ma'am, on Ord Whittaker.'

38

'Sheriff seems t' know what he's doin',' offered Heeney. 'I'd put m' money on his judgement. We'll be rollin' int' Lateness before yuh can blink!'

'You seem very confident, Mister Heeney,' smiled the woman.

'Oh, yes, ma'am, I am—very. Always look on the brighter side is my motto. Yessir! Never any point in lookin' f' night while the sun's still shinin'.'

'Night comes just the same,' murmured Smith.

'That mebbe so, sir, but right now it's sun-up and that'll do f' me. What yuh think, ma'am? Sun-up clear enough f' y'self?'

'I trust a good deal to the fates, Mister Heeney. They seem to have the last word in most cases.'

'That's profound thinkin', ma'am, and no mistake. Shade too deep f' my reckonin'. But I'd wager on that Whittaker gang bein' miles West of here by now. They ain't got no cause t' hang around these parts. Nothin' here f' them, is there?'

'Only us,' said Smith.

'Ar, come on now, mister, we ain't no great catch, are we? Boys like that'll be lookin' f' bigger spoils. I'd reckon a few days in Lateness bein' more t' their likin'. Whisky and wild women—beggin' yuh pardon, ma'am.'

'Then yuh don't know Ord Whittaker,' said Smith.

'Do you, Mister Smith?' asked Leonora Grey.

The man's grey eyes darkened for a moment. 'I got a clear imagination, ma'am,' he murmured.

The stage lurched again and rolled on into the long sprawl of the river valley.

Shake Reams had plenty to concentrate on as he drove the stage through the rough country flanking the south-eastern side of the Toomey. There was this situation to begin with. Sheriff could be right in his thinking of avoiding the main trail, but Cascade Pass was another matter. Driving a stage through the lower reaches of the mountains would be bad enough—it would take time and a deal of cool handling—but then there was the Pass itself: dark, wild and a sight too long for Shake's liking. It would be like picking his way over scattered cacti.

Burying Big John had been another upset. Shake could hardly imagine a time when he and B. J. had not been the very closest of friends. Fact is, he mused, we never did have a harsh word between us. And now he was gone...

And then there was Mrs Grey's luggage, just that one small valise. Hell, the thought of that ate into him! Made no sense. And Smith's face—there was another mystery; them grey staring eyes. Where in tarnation had he seen the critter before?

But there was something else troubling Shake on this morning, something he had seen the night before. He had been crossing from the stabling at the post after settling the horses and thinking that he might just get to finishing the last of the coffee, when he had seen the shadow move across the moonlit window of the room he was certain Mrs Grey was occupying. The shadow of a man. But which man, he wondered, and why had he been in Mrs Grey's room? More to the point, had she known he was there?

Maybe he should say something to the Sheriff when they reached the river. Lou would know what to do...

The noon sun was high and blazing when Shake brought the stage to a slithering halt in the shale and pebble reaches of the River Toomey.

'Well done,' said Benson, jumping down. 'We made good time. We'll rest up awhile, then make the crossing.' He looked round him. 'Seems quiet enough.'

Shake let his gaze range over the soft flow of the shallow, rock-pitted waters, the shimmering glow at the surface where the flow bubbled and bounced and eddied, and the sprawl of the brush country on the far side, climbing steadily to the mountain peaks and Cascade Pass. Peaceful enough, he agreed.

They had lit a small fire and had a pot of fresh coffee close to ready when Cal Heeney put a finger to his lips and urged the others to silence.

'Don't any of yuh turn round,' he whispered. 'Some ways downriver, close t' a break in the rocks—company.'

It was a full half-minute before Lou Benson moved casually from the group at the fire to the head of the team of horses and narrowed his gaze on the distance south-west where the river slid into a long curve. He saw the break in the rocks, a straggling of dead trees, and then, flitting like loose shadows among them, the shapes of two men, crouched now and watching.

'Whittaker's boys f' sure,' said Shake, joining him. 'What the hell they doin' out here?'

Lou continued to watch. The men were typical of Ord Whittaker's gang tactics: two, sometimes three men working as outriders from the main bunch; the eyes and ears that warned of what was coming or who was following. Ord took few chances.

'We movin'?' asked Shake.

'No,' said Benson. 'We wait.'

The waiting in that hot, sun-baked noon

lasted no more than minutes.

The two men, mounted, moved at a slow, easy pace upstream to the stage, their stares fixed and tight on the figures at the fire, their Winchesters gleaming liked raised spears.

'They look as mean as mountain cats,' muttered Heeney as the men came closer.

'Meaner than that, son,' said Smith.

'Howdy,' called Benson cheerfully when the men had halted a few yards short of the fire. 'Coffee's fresh if yuh'd care t' step down.'

The men stayed silent and staring, first at Benson, then slowly over the other faces until their eyes settled hungrily on Leonora Grey.

'She's mine,' mouthed the leaner, scruffier of the pair.

'We share,' snapped the other. 'Me first.'

'Yuh fellas headin' f' Lateness?' asked Benson airily. 'Stage here's been diverted North of High Rivers. We gotta call to make at—'

But that was as far as Lou Benson got

with his words. Two seconds later the noon light seemed to dance in crazy patterns, then rip apart as if no more than a torn sheet of paper. There was a swirl of shale dust as the horses bucked, the roar of a Colt—once, twice in a stream of lead—and suddenly, still and flat and staring through bloodshot eyes, two dead bodies on that once quiet stretch of the River Toomey.

Leonora Grey, Cal Heeney, Lou Benson and Shake Reams turned their heads slowly to gaze at Smith, who simply smiled and holstered his gun.

SIX

'Sonofabitch! Faster than a termite munchin' dirt! Hell, Lou, did yuh see that—did yuh see that shootin'? I ain't never seen shootin' like that before.' Shake Reams lifted his hat and scratched his head, then went back to helping Lou Benson prepare the team for moving.

45

'I seen it,' said Lou flatly.

'Where'd a fella learn shootin' like that? Them critters never blinked. I swear they never blinked. Another half-minute and Mrs Grey might've...' Shake paused. 'This mean the Whittaker gang is close?'

'I reckon,' said Benson. 'Trouble is, where? They could be up ahead. They could be trailin' the river.'

'They could've seen us. Mebbe heard them shots.'

'Mebbe. But we ain't hangin' about t' find out. We'll hide these bodies best we can, scatter the fire and hitch the critters' mounts t' the stage. Then we cross the river, mister, and fast!'

'Yuh got it, Lou!' growled Shake.

There was a pinched, pale look on Leonora Grey's face as she sat motionless in the stage waiting for the first creak of movement. Her stare had not shifted, her hands never moved from her lap. She had not spoken since being helped aboard.

'Yuh feelin' all right?' asked Heeney carefully.

The woman simply nodded.

Heeney turned to Smith. 'Guess we owe yuh our thanks, mister.'

'No thanks needed,' said Smith.

'I wouldn't say that. Them gunslingers weren't foolin'. They'd have taken what they wanted... And I don't need t' spell that out in front to the lady here. Yuh know full well what I mean. Whittaker's men, weren't they? And that means the gang's hereabouts. Hell!' He adjusted his hat and jacket. 'That was some shootin', Mister Smith,' he went on. 'Real fast. I ain't seen nothin' faster—and I seen some, believe me.' He paused, his gaze probing Smith's face. 'Yuh some sorta professional?'

Smith turned his head slowly, his grey eyes bright with the light. 'Professional what?' he asked.

'Gunman,' said Heeney bluntly.

Smith grinned. 'What would you say, Mister Heeney?'

'I'd reckon there's a fair chance yuh are. Fact, I'd say—'

The stage creaked; hooves slithered for a

grip on shale; wheels turned; Shake Reams'
voice rose on the thick, warm air in a
rolling growl.

'We're movin'',' said Heeney. 'Thank
God f' that.'

Leonora Grey's stare settled on Smith.
The man smiled softly at her, but there
was no flicker of response on the woman's
dry, tight lips.

Shake Reams was surprised at the ease
of fording the Toomey. He had expected
deeper water, a sandbed too soft to take
the weight of the stage, unseen snags
below the surface, drifting flotsam. But
there were no such hazards, and within
an hour the stage was drawn up safely on
the opposite bank.

'There ain't much of a trail f' an outfit
this size t' the Banks' homestead,' he
announced to Lou Benson. 'Have t' make
the best of it.'

Benson nodded and settled to concen-
trating on the way ahead, and not least
on keeping a close watch for signs of the
Whittaker gang. The men at the river had

been scouting, no doubt about that, he reckoned. But that deduction raised more questions than it answered. And it also raised the mystery of Mr Smith.

Shake had been right about Smith's ability with a gun. He was fast, too fast for a man who might otherwise have been taken for a quiet, well-dressed banker. His sort of gun handling was professional, but if that were so, who was 'Mr Smith', where did he come from, and why was he here?

Benson had no answers in that hot afternoon air. Only certainty in his mind was that Smith was not heading for Lateness by chance. He was a man with a mission. It showed in his eyes.

Two hours passed at a slow, ponderous pace, with Shake working the team through the difficult terrain to the Banks' place. There were never more than minutes of easy going; times when he had to rein the team back to a standstill, give them time to settle their sweating and gather their feet. Main trouble was, he figured, he could not expect the horses to keep up this effort for much longer. Another

49

hour at most and he would be forced to call a halt.

He reminded himself that it had been close on a year since he last set eyes on George and May Banks. Wintertime, just before Christmas... They had come through to Steeple for one of their rare treats to town. Nice folk... May had reckoned they might be starting a family come the Summer... Some struggle for survival in a country as harsh as this, but George was hard-working and May stood to his side with true heart...

'Yuh smell that, Shake?' called Lou, riding back to level with the stage. 'Yuh catch a whiff of that smoke?'

Shake raised his nose to the faint shift of air and sniffed. 'Wood smoke,' he said. 'Must be closer t' the homestead than we reckoned. I'll wager May is plannin' on an early supper! And I won't be sayin' no t' that!'

Lou Benson sniffed again. 'Some smoke. Mite more than wood if yuh ask me.'

'Soon be knowin'.'

Shake eased the team through a snag of

deep brush, steered them round a sprawl of rocks and reined back with a full, shoulder-wrenching heave at the sight of the destruction that lay below him at the foot of the drift to a narrow valley—a sight that turned his stomach and stiffened his spine with the chill of ice.

'F' crissake!' he mouthed. 'What in hell...'

'Hold it right here,' said Benson. 'I'm goin' down.'

There was only the smouldering shell of the homestead left; bare, gaunt rafters reaching like black fingers to the blue sky; scorched floorboards, a hanging door, the tattered remains of the sparse furniture; scattered utensils, the trappings of an ordinary, everyday life, the smoke curling through them like the breath of ghosts.

And face-down in the ash-blackened dirt, the dead body of George Banks.

Benson squatted at the man's side. He had been shot a half-dozen times in the back. 'Hell!' he cursed, standing upright again.

51

He peered into the twisting shafts of smoke, walked slowly through the charred mess of what had once been a home. No horses around, he noted, no other signs of any life. And where was the woman? He stooped to pick up a torn length of a dress. 'Hell!' he cursed again.

'They play real rough, don't they?' said Smith at Lou's side. 'This explains them louse at the river.' He lifted his gaze to the backdrop of mountains. 'They'll be somewhere up there by now.'

Benson turned the length of dress through his fingers. 'They've taken Mrs Banks.'

Smith's eyes narrowed, glinted as his lips tightened, but stayed silent at the approach of Heeney and Shake.

'Yuh made a real smart decision back there at High Rivers, Sheriff' snorted Heeney angrily. 'Real smart! Yuh realise what yuh done, don't yuh? Yuh brought us right int' the teeth of them Whittaker boys, that's what yuh done! Right int' their Godforsaken teeth, damn yuh!'

'Hold it, mister,' snapped Shake. 'This

ain't no fault of the Sheriff's. We're doin' what we think is right.'

'Right?' scoffed Heeney. 'What's right about draggin' us int' hell? What's right about bringin' a woman t' it? What's right about all this? And what's right about—'

The sudden lift of Smith's arm, the clenched fist that landed squarely on Heeney's jaw, were like flashes of the light. Heeney fell to the ground and had a hand on the butt of his Colt when Smith's boot thudded across his arm.

'Easy, son. Easy. Yuh'll go makin' a string of troubles f' y'self mouthin' off like that,' murmured Smith.

Heeney's face flushed. Smith merely smiled. Benson relaxed again.

Shake Reams spat fiercely. 'Hell, this ain't no time t' be growlin' 'tween ourselves like frettin' wolves. They've taken the woman, ain't they? Taken May?'

'Looks that way,' said Benson.

'We gotta get t' her, Lou,' snapped Shake. 'We just gotta. We owe that t' George.'

'Let's clear up here first,' said Benson.

53

'And somebody had better take care of Mrs Grey. I don't want her t' see what's happened here.'

But when they turned to look at the stage, Leonora Grey was already standing on the rim of the slope, her eyes filled with a deep, darkening fear.

SEVEN

There was a glow of early evening by the time they had buried George Banks and Benson had ordered Shake to drive the stage on a mile or so from the grisly remains of the homestead. They would camp for the night in the cover of a pine spread at the foot of the hills that shelved to the mountain peaks.

'And then what?' Shake had asked. 'We gotta do somethin' about May Banks. We can't just leave her with the Whittaker mob. Yuh got any idea what she's goin' through right now?'

Lou Benson had no need to be reminded of May's fate. 'But the fact is, Shake, we wouldn't stand a chance against the Whittaker guns. We'd like as not all finish up eatin' dirt, and we can't risk that.'

'Yuh ain't goin' t' leave her, are yuh?' Shake had persisted.

'No, I ain't,' Benson had said grimly, 'but we gotta get this outfit through t' Cascade Pass.' He had paused. 'Mebbe Heeney was right. Mebbe I did make the wrong decision back there. Mebbe we should've stayed with the main trail.'

'Wouldn't have made no difference by my reckonin',' Shake had frowned. 'I figure Ord Whittaker's been scoutin' us out since we arrived at High Rivers. He would've caught up with us whichever way we went. Sadness is what we found at the homestead. Just the Banks' bad luck t' be in the Whittakers' path. Them critters don't pass up a woman when they find one. Whittaker probably knows where we are right now. And yuh can bet he's found them sidekicks' bodies at the river. That ain't goin' t' please him none! But yuh can also bet he knows we gotta woman aboard—so now he'll wait till he's ready and then take us. Unless, o'course, yuh got other ideas?'

But Lou Benson had no ideas, only a purpose, and he was sticking with it.

'Another thing,' Shake had begun again. 'I noticed somethin' back there at the post, somethin' I don't figure—'

But in the next moment Leonora Grey joined them from the shadowed area of pines where she had been sipping at a mug of coffee.

'If I might have a word, Sheriff,' she said with a faint smile.

'Sure, ma'am,' said Benson.

'I saw what happened with Mister Heeney at the homestead, and I heard what he said.' Her blue eyes were fixed like moons on Benson's face. 'I'm sorry. Mister Heeney should not have displayed such an outburst. It was unnecessary and untrue. I'm sure you're doing your best for us, Mister Benson, and I for one am grateful. I suggest you dismiss Mister Heeney's comments.'

'Sorry yuh had t' see the place, and what happened,' said Benson. 'But I'm obliged t' yuh f' what yuh've said.'

Leonora Grey smiled softly. 'Good. Meantime, there's a stream just the other side of the trees there. I would welcome a little privacy while I wash.'

'Go ahead, ma'am,' Benson nodded. 'Yuh'll be safe enough, but I'd prefer yuh not t' be too long. I'm plannin' on closin' down the fire just as soon as it's full dark. We need a fresh start from here come the first show of light.'

The woman smiled again. 'I understand. Thank you.' She hesitated. 'I was wondering...' Her smile faded. 'Tomorrow will do.' She gave her skirts a swirl and went back to the shadows.

'Well, now,' grinned Shake, 'ain't that somethin'! Put Mister Heeney right in his place. No messin'! She don't suffer fools lightly, and that's f' sure. Say what yuh like about the woman, Lou, but Sam Grey knew what he was about when he set his eye on her. No mistake.'

Lou Benson simply grunted.

57

'Anyhow,' continued Shake, 'like I was sayin' about what I seen back at the post and still can't figure—'

'Later, Shake,' said Benson. 'Right now we should be tendin' that team. They got one helluva haul facin' them come sun-up. How far t' the Pass d' yuh reckon?'

'T'ain't the miles,' sighed Shake, 'it's the goin'. There's a whole heap of rock and screes after this, then the drop through the creek and no trail worth the name after that. Still, I'd reckon on havin' the Pass in our sights soon after noon, assumin' Ord Whittaker and his bunch don't take it int' their heads...'

The gentle, settled silence of that evening was broken as if splintered by a hammer blow across rock. Where, a moment ago, there had been no more than the shuffle of a close of day breeze, the softest snort from the line-hitched team, there was now the piercing pitch of a scream that seemed to hang on the air like a strangled echo; a sound that broke, lifted, swirled and filled the space with its dread.

58

'Mrs Grey!' shouted Shake.

'The stream!' yelled Benson.

'What the hell was that?' called Cal Heeney, bursting from the shadowed side of the stage.

Lou Benson was ahead of the three men as they tumbled through the pines and down the draw to the twist of stream.

Leonora Grey was on her knees at the side of the flow. The top half of her dress had been torn away, the lower half ripped to shreds to expose the gleam of her thighs, the smooth shape of her buttocks. Her hair was plastered in wet strands across her bare shoulders, her breasts only part covered where she hugged the tattered fabric of the dress to her.

She raised wild, staring eyes to the men as they approached, then turned them back again to the body sprawled in front of her, a knife buried deep between its shoulder-blades.

'F' crissake!' mouthed Shake.

'What the hell—' began Heeney.

'One of Whittaker's men,' added Shake. 'Must've been hidden here, watchin' us.'

Lou Benson stared at the body. 'But who—'

Heeney had reached the woman and was kneeling at her side when Smith stepped from the shadows of the trees, moved to the body and, with his back placed carefully to Leonora Grey, withdrew the knife from flesh and cleaned the blade on the man's shirt.

'I'll be darned!' hissed Shake.

'What happened?' asked Benson.

'I was in the trees takin' a look round, just checkin',' said Smith, 'when I saw Mrs Grey come down the draw t' the stream. I could see what she planned and had turned t' come away when this critter plunged outta nowhere and attacked her. Didn't wanna create a lot of noise, so I used this.' Smith held the blade of the knife to the evening light. He smiled. 'Thought I might've lost m' touch with it. Seems not.'

'Hell!' murmured Shake.

'Looks t' me as if our friend, Whittaker, intended keepin' a watchful eye on us through the night,' added Smith. 'This fella got greedy.'

'Get the fire freshened, Shake,' ordered Benson. 'Mrs Grey's goin' t' need warmth. And find some blankets or somethin'.' He turned to Smith. 'I'm obliged t' yuh, Mister Smith—once again. Gettin' t' be a habit. But thanks, anyhow. That was quick thinkin' on yuh part. Nice throwin' too. Lucky yuh had the knife with yuh.'

'Never without it!' grinned Smith.

Leonora Grey was still pale but more composed once wrapped in blankets before the glow of the fire. The warmth had stilled her shivering and her eyes were brighter, her soft lips without the nervous twitch. There was a faint, flickering smile on them as she eased her gaze to Lou Benson.

'Thank you,' she said quietly. 'And I'm sorry for causing so much trouble. That was not a good idea.'

'Thanks go to Mister Smith. If he hadn't been around...'

'Yes,' replied the woman slowly. 'Of course... Mister Smith. We seem to owe him a lot.'

Benson grinned wryly. 'He's a capable

fella, ma'am. Seems t' know his business, whatever it is.'

'What do you think it is, Mister Benson?'

'No notion, ma'am. I ain't had the time t' ask, nor, come t' that, t' say how sorry I am t' see yuh leavin' Steeple.'

'I'm not sure that I am at this moment!'

'Yuh'll make it, ma'am. Yuh can count on it.' Benson paused. 'Real shame about yuh husband. Didn't have a lot t' do with him, but when I had occasion he seemed obligin' enough.'

The woman's eyes darkened. 'Is there any news yet—about who shot him?'

'Nothin' firm, but I got m' own theories.'

'Oh? Would you care to share them?'

'Too soon, ma'am, but yuh'll know the minute I'm certain. One thing's f' sure, whoever it was ain't goin' t' get away with it. Meantime—'

'Meantime, we seem to have other problems!'

'Yuh, can say that again, ma'am.' Benson came to his feet. 'Take it easy now. Rest up. We gotta big day comin' and I gotta talk t' Shake.'

Leonora Grey's lips had broken to a smile again as Benson moved away, but it had faded by the time her stare was settled on the lick of flames from the fire. She could see a face in them—that same face, the same eyes, beckoning her...

Benson found Shake seated by the stage with Heeney and Smith.

'Mrs Grey'll be okay,' he said. 'She was lucky.'

'Reckon we're runnin' outta luck,' groaned Heeney. 'Whittaker's closin' in, ain't he, sheriff?'

Benson grunted. 'I'm figurin' on a change of tactics.'

Smith blew a long curl of smoke from his cigar and fixed his grey-eyed stare on the sheriff.

'Seems pretty obvious now that Whittaker is intent on takin' us and the stage,' continued Benson. 'He'll reckon on the stage movin' come sun-up. It will—but it'll have only Shake aboard.'

'What?' gasped Heeney.

Smith blew more smoke. Shake frowned and scratched his head.

Benson waited a moment, then went on: 'There's no way Shake'll manage t' get a fully loaded stage t' Cascade Pass, but he might stand a fair chance makin' his own way, at his pace, with an empty coach.'

'And what d'the rest of us do?' snapped Heeney.

'We walk.'

'*Walk!*' Heeney jumped to his feet. 'Walk did yuh say?'

'I said walk, mister.'

'In this heat, in this country, with a woman? Yuh gotta be crazy!'

'No,' said Benson calmly, 'I'm makin' sense. Seems t' me Whittaker'll soon figure we ain't aboard the stage and turn his attention t' trackin' us. With luck, Shake'll make it t' the Pass and, if the rest of us are careful, real careful, and if luck's with us, we'll join up with him and make the run t' Lateness. Point is, Whittaker's mob is goin' t' have t' concentrate on two fronts: us and the stage. We're goin' t' stretch him—and mebbe confuse him.'

'And how far we goin' t' have t' walk?' asked Heeney.

'Twenty miles I'd reckon,' said Shake. 'But yuh'll mebbe shorten that some if yuh work yuh way through the hills. Better cover too. As rough f' whoever's on yuh trail as y'selves.'

'Twenty miles f' crissake!' sighed Heeney.

'But I reckon it might work,' added Shake. 'Lou's right about the stage—I'll make it empty, and once Whittaker knows I'm empty I ain't goin' t' be half as much interest t' him. If yuh can make it to the Pass, I'll be there!'

'What d' yuh reckon, Mister Smith?' asked Benson.

Smith blew another curl of smoke. 'I figure we stand a chance—a better chance on foot than stayin' with the stage. Two movin' targets are a darn sight harder t' hit than one. It's worth a gamble.'

'I ain't a gamblin' man!'clipped Heeney.

'Now's yuh chance t' acquire the habit,' smiled Smith, drawing long and deep on his cigar.

65

EIGHT

It took close on three hours for Lou Benson and Shake Reams to organise their separate departures. The night was still black and silent when Benson finally drew Shake aside.

'I ain't unaware of what I'm askin' of yuh,' he said quietly. 'If Whittaker does decide t' hit the stage and take it—'

'I know,' grinned Shake. 'I'm on m' own! We'll see... Yuh just leave the stage and the team t' me. Make sure yuh make it t' the Pass fast as yuh can. And if yuh see anythin' of May Banks, do the best yuh can f' her.'

They shook hands. 'Pull out soon as it's light enough,' added Benson. 'I'm goin' t' shift the others now. Sooner we're movin', sooner we'll be there.'

He went to find Leonora Grey. She was looking a deal healthier, he thought, and had managed somehow or other to patch together her torn dress.

'Sorry it has t' be like this ma'am,' he said. 'Don't exactly like the idea of yuh havin' t' set foot int' this country, but there don't seem no other way right now.'

'Just as long as we make it to Lateness, Mister Benson,' she smiled. 'That is my only concern.'

'Sure, ma'am,' grunted Benson, then left her to join Heeney and Smith.

'We move out soon as yuh ready. We travel light. Should be plenty of water in the hills. Make sure yuh guns are in good shape. We ain't lookin' f' trouble, but doubtless it'll be stalkin' us.'

A half-hour later Shake watched the group disappear into the cloak of dark trees.

'Good luck,' he murmured to himself, then slapped his thigh in annoyance. 'Heck,' he mouthed, 'never did get t' tellin' Lou about what I seen back at the post. Too late now...'

Cascade Pass lay deep in high country to

the north-west. There were two possible routes to reach it: the first would take the group through the reaches of open country, with no more than scatterings of pines for cover; the second, though longer and tougher, would mean them holding to the hills with its rough tracks, creeks, gulches and draws. Lou Benson chose the second.

They made fast, safe progress in that first hour, thankful for a bright moon, cloudless sky and the starlight. It was Benson's bet that Ord Whittaker and his men were holed up somewhere in the hills close to the stage. There would be no movement from them until first light, or until somebody wondered why the man at the stream had not reported back.

But Whittaker would be in no hurry. He could be at the Pass within hours. He would lose time watching the progress of an empty stage, and only later realise that its passengers were moving on foot. That wasted time would give Benson the edge he needed to be well ahead of the gang. He could only pray that Shake would be left alone to wend his slow, lonely way.

Leonora Grey was holding up well, thought Benson. She was some lady and no mistake, but tough with it. Definitely not a woman to underestimate. Heeney travelled without complaint, a slightly bewildered look on his face as if passing through some dream-state from which he feared he might never wake.

But it was Smith whom Benson still pondered over the most. His handling of a gun, not to mention a knife, suggested a man of some ability, well able to take care of himself, who had been used to doing so for most of his life. But a man with a long past. Just how colourful had that been, he wondered? Or was it so dark that even Smith wanted to leave it behind?

There was the first hint of dawn light when Benson called a halt deep in the cover of boulders.

'Good goin',' he said, scanning the breaking skyline. 'Keep yuh eyes skinned soon as it's sun-up, and stay close.'

'Yuh seen this country before, Mister Smith?' asked Heeney.

'Never,' said Smith. 'Like Mrs Grey here I'm more familiar with other territories.'

'Excepting those to the East,' murmured the woman, raising her eyes and smiling softly.

'Never the East, ma'am,' answered Smith firmly.

'Let's move,' clipped Benson, watching the steady glint in Leonora Grey's stare.

Shake Reams watched his team working at almost walking pace over the rock-strewn stretch of dirt and scrub bordering the foothills. The light was full now, the morning bright with an already fierce sun, the air losing the thin chill of night.

Shake's progress from the pines had been slow—and deliberately so. The stage had been rolling barely twenty minutes when he noticed the rider on the rim of the far hills. A look out, Shake had decided. Well, the longer he could keep him interested the better. An easy pace through the easiest country he could find, and then, when he reckoned the rider had taken his fill of looking, he would halt and have himself a quiet breakfast. Alone.

From there on he would be trusting to his luck that the fellow was not the nosey type and would ride off to report an empty stage trundling north-west. A ghost stage, smiled Shake. Ord Whittaker would do all the figuring necessary after that.

Shake waited another fifteen minutes before reining up the team with a shout a deal louder than was needed. He let the dust swirls settle, climbed down, stretched and yawned. He was careful to open both doors of the stage before squatting in the shade with a flask of water, then he simply gazed over the sprawl of hills and watched the lone rider.

A minute...two minutes, coming up three. The rider hesitated. There was a moment when Shake feared the man might lift his Winchester from its scabbard. He could hardly miss a squatting target clear in his sights...But finally the man moved, swung his mount round and disappeared down the drift of the hills to the West.

Shake wiped the sweat from his brow. So far, so good. It was beginning to look like a safe run to Cascade Pass.

It was a far less promising prospect for Lou Benson. He had been leading the group through the hills for what he reckoned must be four hours, the last two of them in the gathering heat of a scorching sun in a near cloudless sky. The shade was skimpy, the going harsh, the pace beginning to slow, and the Pass as remote as ever.

He had wondered how Shake was making out. Had the ruse of the empty stage worked? Would Ord Whittaker fall for it, and if he did when and where would his sidekicks surface next? At the Pass, before it, or would he just wait for the terrain and the sun to take its toll? If Shake made it to the Pass would the group be there to join the stage and make the run for Lateness? Would there be the chance, the time? Which way were the odds shifting?

Benson called a halt in the slim shade

of the next outcrop. Smith joined him and sat quiet for a moment, mopping the sweat from his face.

'I reckon our friends are out lookin' f' us,' he said without turning to Benson. 'They must've seen the stage and made all the right deductions.'

Benson frowned. 'How come?'

'There's been a couple of critters up there in the hills t' the South f' the past half-hour. Don't reckon they've seen us yet, but it ain't goin' t' be long before they do.'

Benson shaded his eyes and scanned the range. It seemed empty enough, without movement or sounds.

'They could've moved on, o'course,' said Smith. 'Or they could be bidin' their time. Either way, I ain't happy havin' them f' company.'

Benson frowned again. 'What yuh suggestin'?'

'We could try takin' them.' Smith's grey eyes brightened. 'Two less of the Whittaker mob t' be bothered with.'

'Risky and not easy,' replied Benson.

'Most things are and nothin' ever is. Yuh game?'

Benson scanned the hills again. 'How?' he murmured, feeling the cold gleam of Smith's stare on his face.

NINE

The sweat in Cal Heeney's neck was turning colder. He was beginning to fidget more than some about 'Mister Smith', about who he was, why he was here on this Godforsaken run to Lateness; that look in his eyes, the way he fixed Leonora Grey with a stare that never seemed to let go; about his ability to kill so easily, and readily, as if it were second nature to him, or maybe first in his case.

And now the critter was planning something with Lou Benson. They had been huddled together in that patch of shade for darn near fifteen minutes. What were they planning? Some scheme of

Smith's for certain—a professional plan, because Smith *was* a professional. A gun for hire.

Heeney shrugged his shoulders under the cling of sweat. And then there was Mrs Grey. He was beginning to worry a whole lot about her. There was trouble brewing with her, unless...

His thoughts faded as Smith moved and made his way towards him.

'We reckon we got pryin' eyes closing in,' said Smith. 'We're goin' t' try t' do somethin' about it. Yuh with us?'

'Do I have a choice?' asked Heeney.

'None worth mentionin',' grinned Smith. 'Yuh just take care of Mrs Grey. Okay?'

'My pleasure!' smiled Heeney.

Smith turned to Benson and nodded, then slipped away into the cluster of rocks at the back of the outcrop.

'Hell!' mouthed Heeney. 'What now?'

Lou Benson was sprawled flat on the slab of rock that had grown out of the outcrop like a giant tongue. He had a clear view to the South, to the narrow creek immediately below him, the scattering of rocks and boulders beyond it, and then on to the roll of southern hills, the sand and shingle, the sprawl of black shadows.

There was no sign of Smith, but he was down there somewhere with some crazy notion he could flush out the Whittaker sidekicks and maybe beat them into Benson's sights. Maybe he could, thought Benson; maybe not. Ord Whittaker's men were no fools. But maybe that was a fact Smith was already aware of.

Benson sighed, gulped, waited, squinted into the glare of sunlight. Time, this was all taking time...the one commodity they did not have. An hour lost now—maybe more—could be vital in reaching the Pass. Might be better if they took the gamble and moved on, let the sidekicks come to them...

He stiffened at the sudden movement ahead of him; a shape, a body bent double, scuttling through the rocks like an insect. Smith was deep into the creek now, moving quickly, pausing, watching, listening. He had almost reached the far end of it when the first of Whittaker's men, a squat, bull-shouldered sidekick clutching a Winchester, emerged from the cover of a mound of boulders and brought Smith to a slithering halt.

'Sonofabitch!' hissed Benson.

He watched Smith lunge to his left, saw the lift of his arm, the flash of the knife in the sunlight. The blade was buried deep in the man's chest before his finger had time to close on the rifle trigger. The sidekick gasped, stared at Smith and fell back into the boulders as if tossed there on some freak wind.

There had been two men tracking through the hills. Where was the second, wondered Benson, struggling to his knees on the rock slab.

Smith was on his feet again and about to move into the boulders when the dead man's partner jumped him from behind. The pair crashed to ground in a writhing knot of arms and legs. It was then that Benson slid from the rock and plunged into the creek.

He heard the crack of a Colt, an

anguished curse. Smith had rolled clear of the man who had fallen, clutching his shoulder. Benson stumbled on, his own gun drawn and levelled.

The man was on his knees now, a cold stare filling his face, his Colt set to blaze. Benson fired, once, twice. The man fell again, this time blood pouring from his neck. There was a moment when the man's Colt was steady, when he might have fired had there been the strength in his fingers and the images moving towards him not been so blurred. Then he slumped, the gun hand went limp and his eyes widened with a wild glaze.

Smith and Benson reached the man together. They stood over him in silence, watched his mouth open as if seeking a last gasp of air. He began to mouth a word: 'Jeff...Jeffer...Jeffers...'

But Smith's Colt had spat at point-blank range before the man could finish.

Benson turned his head slowly to look at Smith whose grey eyes were steady, unblinking, simply staring.

'Thanks,' said Smith as he made his way along the creek with Benson. 'Yuh moved just in time.'

'Yuh know that critter back there?' asked Benson. 'Seemed like he was tryin' t' tell yuh somethin' before yuh finished him.'

'Never set eyes on him. Just one of Whittaker's mob as far as I'm concerned. One less—two t' be exact!'

Benson shrugged. 'Whittaker's a mite too close f' my likin'. He ain't goin' t' give up now.'

'Mebbe not,' said Smith, 'but he ain't goin' t' hit us yet, either. He'll wait till he's certain where the stage is headin', then strike.'

'Meantime, we tread dirt fast as we can.' Benson paused to wipe the sweat from his face and neck. 'Should put a few miles underfoot before evenin'.'

Smith grunted and strode ahead.

Benson watched him go. He was still thinking about the sidekick who had tried to say something. Smith might never have set eyes on him before. But perhaps the real point was, had the man set eyes on Smith?

Benson's determination to keep up a steady pace through the afternoon produced results. The group cleared the worst of the rough rock country and were approaching the foothills of a new mountain range by the time the sun had slid lower in the already darkening western sky.

Heeney had stayed close to Leonora Grey throughout the long, hot hours of trekking. She had remained stoic but silent, rarely saying more than a demure expression of thanks when offered a helping hand. Heeney had seemed to relish the protective role with a cheerfulness that hardly disturbed the half smile on his face.

Smith was another matter, thought Benson. He too stayed silent, but his eyes were never still in gazes that swept over the country like beams of light. If there was anything out there that did not fit the pattern, he would be the first to know—and maybe deal with it. Benson was happy enough to accept the situation. Right now, Smith, whoever he might be, was worth two men.

There had been no further sight of Whittaker's men and no signs that they were tracking the group. That, Benson guessed, had been the job of the two men now dead at the creek. Maybe Smith was right; maybe Whittaker would wait until they were closing on Cascade Pass. Then what, he wondered?

They had a small fire crackling and coffee brewing when the night shadows began to thicken. Benson waited until Leonora Grey had rested before joining her where she sat apart from Heeney and Smith.

'Yuh did well, ma'am,' he smiled. 'Mebbe the goin' will be a mite easier from here on.'

'I hope so,' she said, returning his smile. 'Were those Whittaker's men at the creek?'

'Scouts, ma'am, keepin' a close watch. Not any longer!'

'Did you kill them, Mister Benson?'

'Smith and me between us.'

The woman nodded. 'There'll be more?'

'Hard t' say. Depends on Whittaker's figurin'.'

She nodded again. 'Perhaps I should get some sleep.'

'Good idea, ma'am. We'll be movin' again soon. Got t' make as much progress as possible.'

Benson took the first watch as the group settled to snatch at sleep. The night air was still warm, and it was maybe its closeness, he thought, that was keeping Leonora Grey awake—that or her concentration on watching Smith as if fearful that he might move.

TEN

Shake Reams had set the stage rolling a good hour before light had broken. The going, he knew, was still rough, but he could handle the team; they were fresh and the empty stage was no strain on them. They should soon be eating the miles left. Given luck, he would have the approaches to the Pass well within his sights in a few hours. All he needed was the blessing of fresh water somewhere between here and the mountains; one of the streams that fed the Toomey. Just a question of keeping an eye open and his nose to the ground.

He set to wondering how Lou Benson was making out...

The morning was breaking, the sun cresting the eastern horizon like a red eye anxious to blink, when Shake first saw the handful of dark shadows ahead of him begin to move. Could be a trick of the light, of course. Just a shift of it. Man tended to see all manner of things come sun-up. Mostly they were the land taking shape.

But these were maybe more than just shadows, he thought, straining to peer through the haze. These could be a half-dozen riders waiting and watching... Waiting for what, and who were they watching?

'Heck!' he groaned. He hardly needed three guesses!

These men were from the Whittaker gang. Must have been close by most of the night. Well, no point in trying to outrun them; no point in doing anything save to keep moving. More important now to stay alive, keep the stage and team intact. Hold the pace steady, the line straight, and start praying!

Lou Benson had wasted no time in covering the ground at a fast rate long before first light. He was reckoning now on Shake being well on his way to the Pass. The timing of meeting up with him and making the hard run for Lateness was crucial. Worst thing that could happen would be for Shake to find himself waiting with nowhere to hold a full team and stage out of sight. Somehow the group had to be at the Pass ahead of him...

Heeney looked fresh and still cheerful as the group headed into the hills. Smith was steady, watchful, which was a deal more than could be said for Leonora Grey. She had not closed her eyes during Benson's watch, and this morning it showed. She was pale, nervy and still eyeing Smith with that same questioning wariness. Why, wondered Benson? What did she see in the man that Benson was missing, or was it something she knew? This was not the time to try to find out.

They were still making good headway by the time the sun was full and the heat of the day beginning to thicken. Another hour, Benson figured, and it would be time...

Cal Heeney went down to a single, whining shot from a Winchester somewhere in the mass of rocks above him. The aim had been expert, clean into the left shoulder.

Smith's hand was already on the butt of his Colt as Heeney fell, Benson's fingers within a whisper of his own gun, when the voice called out:

'Hold it right there, fellas. Not another move, unless yuh want t'see the lady lose her head!'

Benson narrowed his eyes on the rock-mass for the sight of a face, a shape, but for what seemed minutes there was nothing, then suddenly, as if growing out of the emptiness, four men rose from cover and moved slowly down the hillside.

Leonora Grey knelt at Heeney's side staunching the flow of blood from his wound. Smith stood tense and stiff, his grey eyes fixed on the approaching figures. Benson was conscious of a trickle of cold sweat in his neck. All that broke the silence in those moments was the fall and scatter of loose pebbles under the men's crunching footfalls.

The tall, lean leader of the four, a sallow-faced man with sunken cheeks and sharp, bloodshot eyes, cradled his Winchester, and grinned. He gazed carefully over the group, his stare settling on Leonora Grey as she came to her feet.

'Mornin', ma'am,' he said, touching the brim of his hat. 'Sorry about the young fella, but I reckon he'll live.'

The man's gaze moved back to Smith. 'I know yuh from some place, mister?' Smith stayed silent. 'Mebbe, mebbe not, eh? We'll see.' The man stared at Benson. 'And a full-fledged sheriff no less! I got a natural aversion t' sheriffs. They give me the creeps somethin' rotten! Usually I shoot 'em straight off, like yuh would vermin, but I got m' orders t' day. The boss wants to meet yuh.'

'Ord Whittaker?' asked Benson.

'That's our man. Waitin' back there. He's sure lookin' forward to' meetin' yuh all, 'specially y'self, ma'am. Shall we go?'

Shake Reams groaned miserably to himself. It was all a darned useless shame. Just when it was looking as if he might make it—then this, six of the meanest, scruffiest, smelliest critters he had ever had the misfortune to set eyes on. Whittaker's men, three either side of the team and stage taking him to... Hell, where were they taking him, he wondered? Could be almost anywhere, but they were still moving West and that was some consolation.

The sidekicks had said little. All he had to do, they had ordered, was keep quiet, do as he was told, drive the stage where they directed and keep his mind and hands on the job.

Not a deal of choice, he had reckoned. Nothing to be gained by resisting—that would end with him dead in the dirt—but maybe there was everything to be said for staying with the stage. That much he owed to Lou and the others, always assuming they were still alive. Or maybe Whittaker had tracked them and was holding them? If that were so, they might yet need the stage.

Shake took a firmer grip on the reins and called encouragingly to the team.

Lou Benson reckoned they had trekked just short of a half-mile before the sallow-faced leader of the sidekicks called a halt on the high rim of a deep creek that filtered away to a stream. He saw a twist of campfire smoke and could already pick up the stench of bodies that had not greeted water in weeks.

'That's it,' said sallow-face. 'Far as we go. Home's where yuh make it. T'ain't nothing t' do with place.' He grinned and prodded the Winchester into Benson's back. 'Just keep movin', Sheriff. There's a long sleep comin' up, rest assured!'

They were threading their way down the steep-sided scramble of rocks to the bed of the creek when the man in dark clothes, dark hat, pants and boots emerged from the shadows as if sliced from them.

The group paused. The sidekicks acknowledged the man who stood, hands on hips, with a slow smile cracking his weather-creased features. The smile broadened until the man's mouth was open in a long, rolling peal of laughter that echoed through the creek, and then ended abruptly.

'Well, now,' grinned Ord Whittaker, 'ain't life full of surprises!'

ELEVEN

Ord Whittaker was still somewhere in his mid-thirties, a tall, rangy, relaxed man; about as smooth as a rattlesnake basking in the sun, thought Lou Benson, watching him as his piercingly blue eyes moved slowly over the faces of the group.

Double Colts were slung loose at Whittaker's hips; his boots, surprisingly, were shined, his clothes a deal fresher-looking than his sidekicks' outfits, his hat tilted forward against the glare. His height gave him an air of confidence, and his authority as the gang's leader would go unchallenged, Benson reckoned. No one argued with Ord Whittaker, not if they were planning on taking another breath.

Whittaker's gaze dismissed Heeney, settled a moment on Benson, longer still on Smith, and went on to consume every inch of Leonora Grey. She held his gaze without moving, as if reading his thoughts and not relishing any single one of them.

'Seems t' me,' he said, 'we got ourselves a strange bunch here, boys.' The gaze moved back to Heeney. 'Now who, I wonder, is he? Looks like an eastern pup who's lost his way! Still, we can see he bleeds fast enough!' There were faint chuckles from the sidekicks. 'A sheriff, I see. Must be Lou Benson from Steeple. I heard of yuh, Sheriff, but I ask m'self what yuh doin' out here. Not chasin' me, that's f' sure. Yuh smarter than t' do that single-handed. So... And then there's the lovely lady. M'pleasure, ma'am. I can see yuh got class. I gotta real feelin' f' classy women. Know what I mean?' There were more chuckles. 'But best of all,' grinned Whittaker, 'we got ourselves a fine prize, a first-rate humdinger.' His eyes were tight on Smith. 'Who is he, Sheriff? He gotta name?'

'Smith—Mister Smith,' said Benson bemusedly.

'Mister Smith... Mister Smith... Yeah, that figures. He would be a Mister Smith, wouldn't he? Plain and simple. No frills. Typical. It suits him, 'ceptin he ain't and never has been *Mister Smith!* Nossir! I'll do the introductions, shall I?' Whittaker's grin slicked to a half-smile. 'Ma'am, gentlemen, meet the notorious Jefferson Grey, fastest, smartest gun ever t' come outta the East! A mite worn-lookin' these days, but don't let that fool yuh. Yuh retired or somethin', Jefferson?'

Leonora Grey had stiffened after a long shudder. Heeney had simply stared at Smith through his sweat-lathered eyes. Benson felt a chill shimmer across his shoulders. So that was what the dying sidekick had been trying to say! Jefferson Grey! He had recognized him, and that was why Smith had shot him at point-blank range. But the name—Grey! Was the man related to Sam Grey? Was that why Smith had been in Steeple? Visiting Sam? There for a reason? And had Leonora Grey also recognized him? Did that explain her watchful gaze on the man?

'Hell!' mouthed Benson to himself.

'Say this f' yuh, Jefferson,' Whittaker

went on, 'yuh ain't lost yuh touch. Yuh been causin' a lot of trouble f' m' boys since we hit this territory. They don't' take kindly t' seein' their partners die. Guess we'll have t' put that t' rights, yuh reckon?' Whittaker's blue eyes were suddenly brighter, almost dancing with the prospect of a shooting.

Smith stood motionless, his stare steady, not a flicker of emotion on his face. 'Been a long time, Ord,' he said quietly. 'Last time we met yuh were still learnin'.'

Whittaker grinned. 'I learned good, eh? I watched yuh at work, Jefferson—that's how I learned.'

One of the sidekicks stepped forward. 'Let's finish it now, Ord,' he growled to murmurs of approval. 'No point in waitin'.'

'In my time, in my time. We got other things t' do first. Beginnin' now.' Whittaker's grin returned. 'Rope these fellas real tight, but leave the lady t' me. She gets m' personal attention!'

'Well?' said Lou Benson, straining once

again at the rope binding his hands behind him. 'Now what—*Mister Smith?*'

Smith turned his head slowly without easing himself from the boulders in which he, along with Benson and Heeney, had been dumped. 'I'm open t' suggestions,' he said.

Lou's face tightened. 'I'll bet yuh are! And mebbe yuh'll be gettin' them before much longer, but right now some explanations would be a good start!'

'There ain't the time,' murmured Smith. 'And this ain't the place. Just take it that Whittaker's right, I'm Jefferson Grey, Sam Grey's brother. Sam grew up respectable. I didn't.'

'But Mrs Grey recognised yuh?'

'She may have seen me sometime years back when Sam came East and met her. M' brother and I didn't keep exactly close company.'

'So what were yuh doin' in Steeple? And what in hell are yuh doin' here? Yuh got some—'

'Hold it, Sheriff. Don't make a speck of difference now one way or the other what

I'm doin', does it, not while we're trussed and wastin' breath yappin'? We gotta get outta this mess before Ord tires of Mrs Grey's pleasures, and before Heeney here bleeds t' death. The rest can wait, savin' t' say that I know who shot Sam Grey, and why.'

'So do I,' said Lou.

Smith shrugged. 'Then we got somethin' in common, ain't we? Let's just hope we live long enough t' see justice done.'

'Since when has justice bothered yuh?' sneered Benson.

'This matter's family, Sheriff, and that makes the difference. Now let's have some ideas...'

Ord Whittaker looked at the woman seated on the rocks by the stream that twisted through the creek, and liked what he saw. She had soft, fair hair, smooth skin, round, inviting eyes and the sort of figure a man did not miss. True, she was pale and obviously tired, but that did not detract from her feminine sparkle. In another place, at another time, she would be the perfect, well-groomed lady whose glance and gentle smile would intrigue. Mrs Leonora Grey had plenty going for her, he decided, and she knew it.

'So,' said Whittaker, 'I got m'self Sam Grey's widow. Well, now...' He smiled as his blue eyes danced. 'Sam's widow, and Sam's brother in the same bag. Quite a haul! Yuh must've known Mister Smith was Jefferson Grey? Yuh must've met him somewheres, him bein' Sam's brother.'

'Perhaps, at a distance, but I don't recall it,' said the woman. 'My husband certainly never spoke of him. Now I can understand why. Sam was a devoutly religious man and a strong upholder of law and order.'

'Thatso?' grinned Whittaker. 'Guess he must've found his big brother somethin' of a disappointment.' He paused, then came a step closer. 'And now yuh headin' f' Lateness?'

'I have friends there.'

'And then?'

'Nothing is decided, but it is most important that I reach Lateness as soon as possible.'

'Long walk, ma'am,' smiled Whittaker.

'I am not planning on walking, Mister Whittaker.' Leonora Grey's eyes flashed.

'So how yuh goin' t' get there?'

'You're going to take me.'

Whittaker's smile broadened. 'That so? Well, now...'

'I can make it worth your while—in many ways.'

Whittaker kicked a stone into the flow and stared at the circling ripples. 'Keep talkin', ma'am,' he murmured.

'I have money in Lateness. There's a valise of jewellery aboard the stage.' Leonora Grey waited a moment for Whittaker's gaze to settle on her. 'And then there's me. I think I read you well enough, Mister Whittaker.'

'I reckon yuh do at that, ma'am.'

'So have we a deal?'

Whittaker kicked at another stone. 'I ain't seen nothin' of the jewellery or the money, which kinda leaves only y'self.'

Leonora Grey smiled and began slowly to unbutton her dress. Ord Whittaker's blue eyes brightened as if suddenly fired by the sunlight. He moved another step closer to the woman as she came to her feet.

'Hey, boss!' called the voice at Whittaker's back. 'The boys are bringin' the stage in right now.'

TWELVE

'Sorry, Lou,' said Shake Reams, squirming at Benson's side among the boulders. 'Did m' best, but I didn't see no point in tryin' t' outrun them critters. Heck, ain't this just one helluva mess! Trussed up here tighter than roped steers; stage taken; Mrs Grey in Whittaker's hands; Heeney half dead—and Smith turns out t' be a gunslinger! I'd reckon that bein' the real rough end of bad luck!'

'I'd back yuh there,' said Benson, trying once again to loosen the rope at his wrists.

'Any sign of Mrs Banks?' asked Shake.

'Not so far. Most of the gang are

camped at the top of the creek. If she's here, she'll be with them.'

'F' crissake!' moaned Shake. 'We gotta do somethin', Lou. Anythin'!'

'Sit tight,' said Smith, opening his eyes.

'Sit tight!' hissed Shake. 'Where in tarnation is that goin' t' get us? And how's sittin' tight goin' t' help the women?'

'Leonora Grey will do a deal with Whittaker,' Smith went on, closing his eyes again. 'That's her style.'

Shake shook the sweat from his face. 'Deal? What sorta deal?'

'A woman's deal. She wants t' get t' Lateness, and she'll pay any price t' make it. I'd reckon on the stage movin' out before nightfall. That'll be our chance—our only chance.'

'Always assumin' Whittaker don't fill us full of lead first!' murmured Benson.

'That,' said Smith, 'is the gamble.'

'Some odds!' groaned Shake.

Lou Benson stayed silent.

Smith, it seemed, an hour later, was right. Ord Whittaker and his dozen or more sidekicks began loading the stage and making the team ready to roll out long before the sun had dipped behind the western crags of the creek.

Whittaker escorted Leonora Grey to the stage, then ordered for Heeney to be brought aboard and for Shake to take up his position as driver. 'And go easy!' Benson had whispered as they led Shake away. The last to board was May Banks, carried unconscious to her seat by the sallow-faced sidekick.

Finally, when the gang were mounted, Whittaker strolled over to the boulders and faced Benson and Smith, his grin wet with sweat, his blue eyes paler in the haze of the late light.

'Been givin' yuh some careful thought,' he said, scuffing a toecap through the dirt, his fingers tapping the butts of his Colts. 'Could do a number of things in your case. Could shoot yuh both here and now. That'd be easy. It'd also make the best sense. Kinda instinctive in my understandin'. But Mrs Grey back there has put in a plea f' the pair of yuh.

God knows why! A sheriff and a one-time fast man with a gun! World would get along well enough without either of yuh! Still, a lady's askin' and the pleasures she promises ain't t' be disregarded. Yuh'd agree? Right? Good, thought yuh would.'

Whittaker walked round them. 'So, here's how I figure it. I'm takin' the stage through t' just short of Lateness. Where I go after that ain't no concern of yours. Mrs Grey is placed similar. She's got her plans, and mebbe she and me'll be ridin' t'gether, so t' speak. As f' y'selves, I'm leavin' yuh right here, just as yuh are—trussed, no food, no water, no weapons, no mounts. Now, knowin' you, Jefferson, there's a fair chance, fifty-fifty, that yuh might just get outta the difficulty, but by then I reckon I'll be clear of Lateness and gone again. Fair? It's fair. And a deal more than m' better sense warns, but if I can't take yuh in a straight shoot, old man, I wouldn't wanna cheat.

'I'll turn the driver loose at Lateness, providin' he's done his job. Same goes f' the homestead woman, if there's anythin' worth turnin' loose by then. M'boys have big appetites! As f' the smart young fella—well, mebbe he'll live, mebbe he'll just bleed t' death. I ain't fussed.'

Whittaker's hands slid away from his Colts. 'Shame yuh didn't get t' know yuh sister-in-law a mite closer, Jefferson. Yuh'd have found her a real delight!' He grinned. 'M' regards, Sheriff. Better luck next time!'

And then he turned and walked away.

Ten minutes later, the stage and the Whittaker gang pulled out of the creek heading West, to leave Smith and Lou Benson with the silence of sundown.

It took Lou Benson a half-hour to make his way from the boulders to the far side of the creek where the gang had been camped. It was maybe a crazy notion that had buzzed through his head in the failing light, some desperate grasp at survival that had gnawed at him as he watched Smith lapse into a fitful, exhausted sleep. But hell, he thought, stumbling for the third time over the jumble of rocks, his hands still securely bound behind him, it was worth a try!

'If yuh don't darned well try...' he gasped, losing his footing and slithering into a crevice. 'If yuh don't try...

And then he was on his feet again, the sweat oozing from him like the frothing of a stream in flood. But on his feet... On his feet and moving down there...to the far side of the creek...to the fire...the ashes of it...the embers the sidekicks had failed to scuff out...

Maybe there was still a glow...just enough to start loosening the rope...scorch through the strands... Just enough...

Maybe...

Sand had been scattered over the remains of the fire sure enough, but there was still the fading glow of embers. He positioned himself as close to them as he dared and settled to wait. Now it was a matter of time and pain...

Time and pain...

His thoughts began to wheel on the night like dark, silent hawks...

Where was the stage; how was Shake

making out; Mrs Banks, Heeney? Why had Leonora Grey struck a deal with Ord Whittaker? What was Whittaker's plan? Where had his thinking taken him? How much did he know? And what had Smith in the back of his mind? Thoughts of revenge for the death of his brother?

Who had really shot Sam Grey?

The shadows had merged into darkness when Benson finally felt the rope beginning to give. The sweat stood proud and gleaming on his face, his wrists were a blaze of scorched flesh, his body taut with the effort and the searing pain. Another few minutes, another tug...

Freedom came with a low groan and sigh, then a call to Smith and a stumbling scramble back to the boulders.

'Lucky f' us they'd had a fire,' said Benson, freeing Smith.

'Lucky, but mebbe anticipated.' Smith's grey eyes shone. 'Yuh don't imagine Whittaker didn't figure on us breaking free, do yuh? He'd reckon on it, bet yuh life, and somewhere out there are a couple of critters who'll finish the job as he planned.'

'What yuh mean?' asked Benson.

'I mean Ord Whittaker don't bargain with nobody, 'specially where we're concerned. Sure he'd strike a so-called deal with Mrs Grey, but he has no intention of keepin' to it. Same as he won't let Shake live, or Mrs Banks and Heeney, and mebbe not Mrs Grey once she's served her purpose.'

'Why'd she want us t' live? We both know—'

'That is somethin' I ain't figured,' said Smith, massaging his wrists. 'Unless... Unless she reads Ord Whittaker a deal sharper than we think. Mebbe she reckons that if we're alive and free, she has a built-in insurance against Whittaker killin' her. She'll know that if we make it outta here we'll head f' Lateness, and that could keep Whittaker occupied while she slips quietly away.'

'Hold on,' said Benson. 'How come yuh seem t' know so much about what Mrs Grey will do? Seems t' me—'

'Don't let's waste time gettin' int' detail,' snapped Smith. 'All we gotta do is stay alive. Like I say, Whittaker'll have fixed f' a couple of his boys t' head back here t' finish us off, and they ain't goin' t' be keen on hangin' about. We ain't got no weapons, no horses, but we do have the night. And that's what we gotta use.'

Lou Benson gazed over the now darkened creek. 'Mebbe we should get t' thinkin'.'

'And then doin',' said Smith coldly.

THIRTEEN

Smith's first suggestion was that he and Benson should leave the area of the boulders and make for the creek's higher ground.

'We're goin' t' need a vantage point as close t' where Whittaker left us as possible,' Smith had said. 'We ain't goin' t' be able t' see a deal, but that works both ways—neither are the fellas sent t' finish us. That evens things up a mite.'

106

Benson reckoned that Shake would get the stage as far as the entrance to Cascade Pass by nightfall. Progress from there come sun-up would be slow, and maybe Shake would do his best to keep it that way. If there was any luck going for them and they could ride out of the creek, there was a chance they could be into the Pass no more than a few hours behind the gang.

But meanwhile, he thought, peering into the darkness from the ledge they had reached overlooking the boulders, there were two killers out there anxious to get their business over...

Benson and Smith had been settled, silent and watchful, in the darkness for nearly an hour when they heard the first clatter of hooves along the western reaches of the creek.

'Here they come,' whispered Benson.

Smith grunted. 'Don't move till they're below us, then take the one nearest yuh. And the best of luck!'

The sidekicks hitched their mounts some distance from the boulders and approached the area on foot. Benson saw them as only vague, shadowy figures scratched on the darkness; faceless, moving like ghosts through the night. There was a moment when they stopped; seconds of low murmurings; surprise and then confusion as they stared at the empty space before them; more seconds of indecision, of debating what to do, where to search, if and when to leave, of facing Whittaker's rage.

Smith and Benson dropped from their cover like dark, hunting hawks. Benson hit the ground to the left of the sidekick he had chosen to tackle, and without waiting to be sure of balance kicked out viciously, his boot thudding into the man's forearm to send his drawn Colt clattering into loose stones.

The sidekick spun round, lashed out at a shape he could barely see, came forward and tripped over Benson's outstretched leg. He sprawled face down in the stones, slid into dirt, rolled and clawed savagely at empty air.

Benson rushed the man as he staggered to his feet, catching him full on the jaw with a swinging punch. The sidekick went down again, this time falling backwards into brush.

Benson charged on, his body filled with the animal instinct for survival, his nerve-ends tingling. The man scrambled out of the tangle of growth, crawled a yard and was turning again when Benson's only weapon, his boot, crashed into the man's cheek, drawing an instant spurt of blood. There was an agonised groan, a flash of eyes, wide and white, and then the man was tumbling into the darkness, slithering helplessly down a slope that ended in another heap of boulders. He hit them with a sickening thud; there was the snap and crack of bone, another groan.

Benson stood over the man, sweat dripping from his chin, his eyes misty with effort. The sidekick did not move. The Sheriff swung round, wiped his eyes and peered through the night for a sight of Smith. There was nothing. No movements, no sounds.

'Smith!' he called, and was answered instantly by the single blaze of a Colt.

Three seconds later, Smith walked out of the darkness, a smoking gun in his right hand. He reached Benson and stared at the man in the boulders.

'He dead?' he asked.

'Mebbe,' gasped Benson, struggling to get his breath.

Smith grunted, raised the gun to his hip and fired twice. The man twitched only once.

'He is now,' murmured Smith, then walked casually away to where the sidekicks' mounts were hitched.

Cal Heeney eased himself into a more comfortable position in the corner of the stage, winced, listened for a moment to the laughter of Whittaker's sidekicks, then closed his eyes on the night and went back to his thoughts.

They were the same as they had been for the past two hours; thoughts of Leonora Grey, Ord Whittaker, the mysterious Mister Smith who had turned out to be Jefferson Grey, Sheriff Benson and this whole damned, tangled mess. More important, how it was ever going to be resolved. Hell, he had been in some scrapes in his time, survived on his wits and luck, but this situation took some beating! And a painful shoulder wound into the bargain.

He sighed. He could imagine what Mrs Grey was doing right now, imagine it in graphic detail. Well, maybe she was right. Maybe it was all she could do. Maybe, like any gambler, she had to play the hand as it was dealt. Even so...

But why had her brother-in-law been in Steeple? What had brought him there? Had Sam Grey contacted him? Had Leonora Grey recognised him? And what was Benson doing in these parts? Why had he ridden out to High Rivers in the first place, and why had he insisted on staying with the stage? Would he and Smith manage to stay alive?

Would he stay alive, he wondered, with a sudden shudder? You hardly had to be a genius to fathom what was in Ord Whittaker's mind.

And now—what now? They were holed up for the night at the entrance to the

Pass. Tomorrow they would begin the haul through it, and soon they would be within reach of Lateness. That would be the time for Whittaker to make his move.

There was another peal of laughter from the sidekicks. They were having what passed for them as fun with Mrs Banks. She, for one, would be glad to see the sun come up. For others it might not be such a welcome sight.

Leonora Grey was hardly conscious of Ord Whittaker at her back where she sat apart from the others in the shadows of a rock outcrop. The air was warm and still, the moon bright in the blackness of unbroken sky, the night close and strangely protective in its depth. She was staring straight ahead, but not at the Pass or the ragged trail through it, not even at the shapes created by the darkness. She was watching the face, that same face that had come to haunt her.

The face of Jefferson Grey.

And he was watching her, a soft grin at his lips, his grey eyes shining in the haze of white light surrounding him. He was haunting, and there was no escape. A face from the past she had seen only once before; somewhere back East when she had first met Sam Grey. Only once, but he might have been with her for a lifetime.

Would he stay with her forever?

She felt Ord Whittaker's hand on the back of her neck, a rough, insensitive hand, but she did not move or resist the probing touch.

'That's a fine collection of jewellery yuh brought along, ma'am,' said Whittaker. 'Worth a fair deal, I'd reckon. I'm obliged.' She could imagine the man's smile. 'That and the money yuh promised should keep me and the boys happy f' some months. I like t' keep the boys happy.' His hands moved slowly to her shoulder. 'By m' reckonin' that leaves only the personal side of our deal—y'self.'

The grin on the haunting face of Jefferson Grey had turned to a smile. The grey eyes were brighter, sharper, boring into her.

'But I guess there ain't no rush on that

score,' murmured Whittaker. 'It's a long time till sun-up.' The hand moved again.

Perhaps Jefferson Grey was already dead, thought the woman. Whittaker had sent men back to the creek. She had seen them ride out. No need to guess at their mission. But if Grey and Benson were dead, that might mean...

The hand slid into her dress, moving to her breast. Leonora Grey closed her eyes on the face, but now she could hear the haunting laughter, mocking, echoing deep into the Pass on that still night air.

She shivered only once as the hand moved on.

FOURTEEN

The light was stirring through a soft pink haze; a slow light already promising high sun and a dry, hot day to come. Soon it would break across the higher peaks and crags, shimmer through the reaches of sand

and outcrops, move on until it was full and gleaming, easing away the cool chill of fading night and early dawn. A time, thought Lou Benson, trailing a mount's length short of Smith, when a man might look forward and not ride in fear of what lay ahead.

Benson sighed, blinked, shook his head, cleared the drift of sleep from his eyes and focused again on Smith's back. They had made good progress through the night, moving quietly westwards towards Cascade Pass on the sidekicks' mounts. The horses were good stock—doubtless stolen, thought Benson—and the weapons the men had been carrying cleaned and fully loaded with an ample supply of spare ammunition. The prospects, he reckoned, were a deal brighter. At least they would catch up with Ord Whittaker and the stage, and, more importantly perhaps, with Leonora Grey. But after that...

His thoughts drifted away as he saw Smith indicate for him to rein up beneath the overhang of a sprawl of rock face.

'Whittaker'll be on the move at first

light,' said Smith, sliding from his saddle to stretch his limbs. 'We're mebbe no more than an hour behind him. So, what's yuh plan when we reach the Pass?'

'Not a lot we can do save trail the stage and wait f' Whittaker t' make his moves. Two of us ain't goin' t' rate much of a chance against him and the gang, but it's m' bettin' right now that he ain't got too much of a notion f' settin' foot in Lateness too soon. I'm figurin' he'll—'

'Kill Heeney, Shake Reams and Mrs Grey once he's got all he wants from them,' said Smith flatly. 'Mrs Grey'll be the last. She's the final pay-off.'

'Pay-off?' said Benson frowning. 'How'd yuh reckon on that? Or is that mebbe lettin' me in on how yuh figure in all this? What yuh were doin' in Steeple, why yuh here, what yuh know about Mrs Grey? Jefferson Grey retired from the scene years ago—that much I do know—so why have yuh come out of retirement? What was so important t' yuh t' spark that, *Mister Smith?*'

Smith ran a hand over his face, adjusted

his hat, settled his feet in the dirt, and grinned. 'Like I said before, *Mister Benson*, we ain't got the time f' talkin'. And I don't reckon yuh goin' t' tell me what yuh doin' out here, anyhow, so I figure we're just goin' t' have t' trust each other till this is over. Right?'

'Time was when trustin' t' the word of Jefferson Grey was like takin' a rattler t' bed!'

Smith's grin broadened. 'But Jefferson Grey retired, Sheriff. Remember?'

Benson's eyes narrowed. 'Yeah...so I heard,' he said slowly.

Shake Reams was in no mood to face a day of the long haul through Cascade Pass. He was also confused. Why in tarnation was Ord Whittaker so keen to get the stage through the Pass, to even stay with it? Why not abandon it now? What the hell did Whittaker want with a stage and full team, anyhow? Shake had no answers, save that while ever the outfit was still in his hands, he was holding on to it. Yessir!

And what had happened to Lou Benson

and Smith? The sidekicks who had ridden back to the creek had only one purpose in mind. So much for Ord Whittaker's word on a deal! And then there was the problem of the Sheriff's reason for tracking the stage in the first place. Had Sam Grey's killer been aboard when they had pulled out of Steeple? Heeney, Smith—Mrs Grey?

'Hell!' cursed Shake above the creaking roll of the stage.

But behind Shake Reams' confusion was his boiling anger. Never mind the treatment being meted out to Mrs Grey, Heeney and himself, it was the degradation May Banks was suffering that seethed within him. If he ever had two free hands again and just half a chance to use them...

Shake called loudly to the team as Whittaker drew his mount alongside him.

'This the fastest we can go?' he asked.

Shake spat into the dirt. 'This is fast, mister, yuh can take it from me. As fast as we're goin' t' go if yuh wanna get this outfit through t' Lateness. And I can't rightly figure why yuh'd wanna do that, either. Don't make a mite of sense t' me, that's f' sure. In fact, I'd go s' far as t' say that yuh just plain—'

'All right! All right!' snapped Whittaker. 'Just drive, will yuh!'

Sure, smiled Shake to himself, at my pace, in my time!

Cal Heeney watched Leonora Grey as she slept in a corner seat of the bouncing stage. She looked exhausted. Her face was drawn and pale, her lips dry, her hair untidy and hanging like weeds, and there were fresh bruises on her neck. She had hardly spoken since climbing aboard the stage at sun-up. Her greeting to him had been no more than a flicker of her lips, a soft, glazed glance through tired eyes. She had no reason to speak, he figured. Her appearance said it all.

What he would have liked to ask her was what she reckoned Whittaker planned to do with the stage; what he planned to do with them, and when—and what had happened to her valise? But maybe the questions would have to wait. Maybe there would be another time, if time was not already fast running out.

Meanwhile, there was his own neck to start thinking about. If he had not taken that shot in the shoulder, if only the pain in it would ease, if this darned trail were not so rough...

The stage bounced again and creaked ominously. There was a sudden, louder creak that ended in a violent crack, a curse from Shake Reams. The stage lurched to one side, scraped over rock and came to a shuddering halt.

Shake let loose another curse. Whittaker and his sidekicks shouted in confusion. Horses snorted and whinnied. Heeney winced, but when he opened his eyes again, Leonora Grey was awake. She glanced bemusedly round her for a moment, then smiled softly, a faint, knowing smile, almost as if the collapse of the stage had been expected and was right on time.

'T'ain't no use! I'm tellin' yuh straight, mister, that axle is cracked. Try movin' this outfit one more yard and the whole thing'll splinter t' nothin'. And that's a fact!' Shake Reams stood back from the stage and stared defiantly at Ord Whittaker.

'Yuh can fix it?' snarled Whittaker.

'Sure I can fix it. Just build me a fire, find me the tools, a spare axle and give me a half-a-day and she'll be good as new!'

Whittaker's blue eyes darkened. Shake stood his ground, waiting for the thud of a fist in his face, or maybe worse, then relaxed as Whittaker turned to one of his sidekicks.

'Change of plan,' he announced grimly. 'We split up.'

'Split up?' mouthed the sidekick. 'But, Ord, yuh said as how—'

'I know what I said, dumbhead, but things've changed, ain't they? This stage ain't goin' no place right now, and I ain't got the time or inclination to hang around while it's fixed. So we split up. Me and some of the boys'll go on t' Lateness and get the business side of things over. Mrs Grey comes with me.

Yuh pick y'self three good men and stay here.'

'What in hell for, Ord?'

Whittaker sighed. 'In case it's escaped yuh notice, our boys ain't back from the creek, are they? They ain't shown. Now, why ain't they shown?'

The sidekick shrugged. 'I guess—' he began.

'Yuh don't need t' guess!' snapped Whittaker. 'It's obvious why they ain't shown. They ain't alive t' show, are they? Jefferson Grey and that Sheriff must've got the better of them. Might've known it. Should've fixed them when I had the chance. Still... So, what d'yuh reckon the pair of them will do now? I'll tell yuh. They'll come trailin' this stage—and you, friend, are goin' t' take care of them. Yuh goin' t' pick 'em off the minute yuh catch a sight of them. Okay? Yuh got it? And yuh can do the same f' the rest of this mangy lot if yuh've a mind. I don't give a damn! Just don't let there be any mistakes.'

'Okay, Ord, okay. I got it. Yuh the boss.'

'Too right I am!'

Whittaker turned again to Shake. 'Yuh get t' work on this outfit best yuh can. I'd prefer it t' roll again. Right? Yuh understand me? If yuh in any doubt, we'll settle it now.' He tapped the butts of his Colts.

'I'll do what I can,' murmured Shake.

Minutes later, Whittaker, Leonora Grey and the gang had ridden out, leaving Heeney, Shake and May Banks in the charge of the four sidekicks. The morning sun was high, the heat beginning to thicken.

Shake wiped the sweat from his face. Maybe Whittaker was right; maybe Smith and Lou Benson had made it out of the creek; maybe they were heading this way... He stared into the shimmering haze of the sand, rocks and hills. This was going to be some day, he reckoned!

FIFTEEN

'He's gone, darn it! He's pulled out!'

Lou Benson slid from the rim of the rock ledge and stared at Smith where he sat with his back to a boulder.

'Looks as if Shake's done his best t' foul up the stage,' he went on, 'but Whittaker ain't there, nor is Mrs Grey. What the hell's he playin' at?'

'I'd reckon he's headin' fast f' Lateness right now,' said Smith, stretching his legs into the sand. 'And Mrs Grey is his ticket t' some hard cash.'

'What yuh sayin'? I don't see that.'

Smith leaned back. 'I'll tell yuh later, but yuh can be certain that Whittaker's figured the sidekicks he sent t' finish us didn't make out. But he knows we'll follow the stage and stop when we reach it—which is precisely what we've done! Now Whittaker's bankin' on his men out there either wipin' us out or pinnin' us down till he's all through in Lateness.'

Benson tipped the brim of his hat against the sun's glare. 'We gotta find a way of takin' that stage—and like soon.'

Smith wiped a lather of sweat from his face. 'Four guns out there with the stage f' cover—and three hostages in their pockets! Don't look good. They'll kill 'em if they have to, make no mistake about that.'

'I know it,' sighed Benson, 'but there's gotta be a way.' He climbed back to the rim of the ledge and gazed over the scene to the mouth of the Pass. 'And mebbe there is,' he murmured. 'Mebbe...'

He dropped back to the shade and sat at Smith's side. 'I see it like this,' he began. 'Won't be long before Shake gets busy with puttin' right whatever's foulin' the stage, and he ain't goin' t' manage that single-handed. He's goin' t' need the help of them sidekicks. Once he's got them workin', we move in. I'll take the left, yuh take the right.'

'Always assumin' them critters feel like workin' and we don't miss!' grinned Smith from beneath his hat.

Benson nodded. 'Always assumin' that,' he agreed.

Shake Reams watched the sweat drip from his chin to the sand and spread like blots of black ink. Hell, it was hot! He stood back from the damaged stage and mopped his brow. It was time to start stalling, he reckoned; time to keep Whittaker's sidekicks occupied with something better than leering at May Banks; time to hope that Lou Benson and Smith were somewhere close and waiting their chance. Time to give them that chance...

'Hey, yuh fellas!' he called to the sidekicks gathered a few yards from where May Banks crouched, shivering in the shade of the stage. 'I'm goin' t' need some muscle here. Yuh'd best get yuh sleeves rolled up and some spit on yuh hands!'

The men did not move. One spat, another smiled cynically, another turned his back on Shake, the fourth posed lazily on one hip.

'Suit y'selves,' shrugged Shake. 'But don't hang it on me when Ord gets back and finds this hulk still sittin' right where it is. He's sure goin' t' get heated over that, and I wouldn't wanna be in your boots—'

'Stow it!' said the man who had spat. 'We get yuh point. What yuh want?'

'Hands,' said Shake, spitting into his own. 'And I wanna fire, good and hot, raked clean to embers. But first, I want yuh shoulders. We're goin' t' have t' lift this baby. Suggest yuh get Heeney out and everythin' unloaded from topside.'

The four men looked at each other, shrugged and strolled towards Shake, whose eyes had suddenly brightened. But he hid his smile.

It was another hour before the long pall of smoke from the sidekicks' fire climbed into the still noon air. Lou Benson watched it from the rim and gestured for Smith to join him.

'That's goin' t' be a help,' he murmured.

Smith grunted. 'Give them a while

longer, then we'll hit them when they're really sweatin'!'

They waited, watching the smoke, the men's efforts to lift the stage, listening to Shake's shouted orders, his curses, the grunts and groans of the sidekicks, and turned their gazes occasionally to the pathetic figure of May Banks, the slumped form of Cal Heeney as he tended his wound.

Would Whittaker return, wondered Benson? How long before he did? Would he make it back to the stage by nightfall, or would he wait for the first light of a new day? Maybe he had other plans—for himself and Leonora Grey. And what had Smith meant by Mrs Grey being Whittaker's ticket to hard cash?

'Now!' hissed Smith.

They slid from the rim, mounted up and walked their horses silently to the edge of the rock cover.

'I'll take the open side away from the smoke, and no arguin', said Benson. 'Plan is t' draw their fire and then yuh follow up on the other side. Okay?'

'Yuh callin' the shots, Sheriff,' shrugged Smith.

'Let's move!'

Lou Benson broke cover at a fast, swinging gallop that raised a cloud of dust and ripped into the hot, dry ground like a sudden shiver of thunder. He gave the mount a free head and slung himself low into its neck, a Colt tight in his right hand.

It was seconds before the sidekicks stopped in their efforts with the stage and turned to face the oncoming rider, still more time for them to shade their eyes against the glare, peer into the dust cloud and be certain that the rider was not one of their own gang. But by then Lou Benson's Colt was already blazing.

The four sidekicks scattered, two fanning out towards him, two tumbling into the cover of the stage. Benson's guns roared again, this time dropping the sidekick nearest to him. There was a crackle of shots from the stage, the blaze of a Colt from the man still running into Benson's path. Hell, he thought, things were a mite too hot already!

He needed Smith—and now!

The sidekick ahead of Benson had dropped to one knee, his gun levelled in a steady, fearless aim. Benson brought his mount round in a swirling change of direction, bucked him hard so that the horse rose on its hindlegs, nostrils flared, eyes wild, and snorted like a demon turned loose. Benson let rip a yell, the mount whinnied, the sidekick came unsteadily upright on the swirl of dust and stone, his gaze lost in the flurry of movement, the burst of noise.

The man's eyes danced as he panicked for a clear sight of his target; the sweat beaded on his unscrubbed face; his lips were suddenly dry, parting in a growl—a growl that was finally lost on the roar of Benson's rapid shots that opened the man's chest as he spun, stumbled three steps and then was face-down and still in the dust that swirled over him like a sullen cloud.

Benson steadied the mount, turned it, pulled back on a tight rein and peered through the sun-streaked grey haze to the stage. His eyes were stinging under the pierce of dust, his skin hot and sticky, his shirt clamped to his back in a lather of sweat.

Smith—where was Smith?

Benson brought the mount on a pace, peered, reined in again. Guns blazed in scattered, aimless shooting from the stage. Cal Heeney's body was covering May Banks protectively; Shake was flat on his stomach, spitting dust; the remaining sidekicks grabbing what cover they could find, one snuggled close to a wheel, the other squirming clear of the stamping hooves of the team.

Benson came on again, wondering now if he could draw the sidekicks' fire from this position—wondering too if he could drop two men before one or both got him.

Smith! Hell, where was he—

He came slowly, loosely through the dust swirls in a blur of shimmering shapes. There was no sight of his face, only the gleam of those grey eyes. His hands were

131

easy on the reins. The tack jangled, the mount snorted. The sidekicks' guns blazed, but the blurred, dust-shrouded rider came on in that same eerie jangle, at the same measured, almost soundless pace, until his darkness filled the space.

And then his Colt spat, once, twice...four shots, two to the left, two to the right; fast, ear-splitting roars that left vicious echoes tumbling through the Pass like the mocking laughter of ghosts.

When the dust had settled and the sun was bright and burning again, the silence gathered as if to watch. Smith glanced quickly at the two men he had shot, and smiled softly to himself.

SIXTEEN

Shake Reams mopped the dust-crusted sweat from his brow and licked his lips. 'Say what yuh like, that was cool shootin'. Cool and calculatin'. Smith ain't no stranger t' that sorta killin', that's f' sure. And if that's Jefferson Grey in retirement, I hate t' think what he must've been like when he was workin' full-time!'

Lou Benson took another swig of water from the flask. Shake was right. Seeing Smith ride in as he had, seemingly unaware of the shots directed at him, had been a haunting vision, almost as if it had not been a horse and rider approaching, but the ghosts of them.

And since then, Smith had remained silently remote. His only concern, it seemed, had been to look to the horses.

'Strange fella,' murmured Benson. 'Just wish he'd get t' speakin' his mind on what he knows, why the hell he's here—and who, in tarnation, he's watchin'. But right now, we gotta heap of other things t' consider. Mrs Banks and Heeney. How are they?'

'Mrs Banks is in a pretty bad way, I reckon. We just gotta get her t' some comfort before much longer. As f' Heeney, he'll live okay. Wound ain't bleedin' nothin' like as much, but I ain't sure what's passin' through his mind. Maybe we should be thinkin' more about Mrs Grey and what's happenin' t' her in Lateness. Don't figure that woman, and that's a fact. Wouldn't care t' say what sorta game she's playin'.'

'F' high stakes,' murmured Benson.

Shake lifted his hat and scratched his head. 'Beats me, but like yuh say, Lou, we got other things t' consider.'

'Movin' this stage f' one thing. How bad's the damage?'

Shake grinned gently, 'Hardly worth mentionin'! Looks bad, but Ord Whittaker don't know nothin' about stages! I rigged this little upset t' slow us down. Figured yuh might've made it outta the creek and guessed yuh'd be headin' this way.' His grin broadened to a smile. 'Don't worry, Lou, we'll have this outfit rollin' again in no time at all.'

Benson slapped Shake's shoulder. 'Good thinkin'. Question now is, where d' we go from here? Can't head straight f' Lateness. Whittaker's boys'd hit us long before we got

134

anywhere near it.' He paused, scratching his chin. 'We need t' just disappear, leastways f' the next few hours. Any ideas?'

Shake was silent for a moment. 'There's a canyon up ahead,' he mused.

'Touch Canyon? But yuh'd never—'

'I know. T'ain't exactly a feather-beddin' ride—too darned narrow f' m' likin'—but I reckon I could make it. Ain't no other place. We gotta give it a try.'

Benson gazed down the long sprawl of the Pass. If Whittaker was intending on returning to the stage, they had only a few hours to leave him guessing where the outfit had disappeared to; maybe no more than the hours left to nightfall. Touch Canyon looked like the only choice.

'Okay,' he said, turning to Shake. 'We get Mrs Banks and Heeney aboard, load up and move out. I'll tell Smith what we're plannin'. He ain't got no choice, either.'

Cal Heeney reckoned that life had taken a turn for the better. His luck was in and holding. The pain in his wound had eased, the bleeding been staunched, the stage was rolling again; Sheriff Benson and Smith were back from the dead—and he knew exactly where Leonora Grey was and who she was with. Not bad, not bad at all, he thought, lounging almost comfortably in the stage's corner seat.

All he needed now was for Benson and Shake to get the stage through to Lateness, and for Smith to stay his distance...

May Banks' stiff stare into nowhere broke on a sudden jolt of wheels over rock and a loud curse from Shake Reams. She rolled to her right, put out a hand and felt it firmly safe in the warm grip of the man seated opposite her.

'Steady,' smiled Heeney. 'This ain't no easy ride, ma'am, in more senses than one!' The smile broadened. 'Name's Heeney—Cal Heeney. Pleased t' meet yuh, Mrs Banks.' The smile faltered, failed and disappeared. 'Sad circumstances,' he added. 'I'm real sorry about...' He paused. 'Yuh feelin' a mite better, ma'am? I did m' best f' yuh back there, but what with this shoulder an' all, well, I guess it weren't much.'

'I'm grateful t' yuh, Mister Heeney,' said the woman. 'Real grateful...' Her brown eyes brightened for a moment, then faded back to their stiff stare, this time fixed on Heeney's face. 'Yuh do somethin' f' me, mister?' she asked.

'Sure, if I can,' grinned Heeney.

'Kill 'em—kill them bastards who took m' man! Yuh do that f' me?'

Heeney paled. 'Ord Whittaker...'

'Them men. All of 'em. Every last critter! Will yuh? If yuh don't, I will! Just as soon as we get t' Lateness.'

Heeney felt the woman's hand turn icily cold. 'Sure,' he said gently. 'Sure thing, Mrs Banks. Yuh just leave it t' me...'

May Banks' brown eyes darkened and her stare settled without a blink.

Heeney sighed. He had a feeling Mister Smith had already taken the same matter into his mind...

'How we doin'?' called Lou Benson, reining his mount alongside the stage.

'Fine, just fine,' shouted Shake, urging the team to smoother ground. 'Should sight the Canyon in an hour. Yuh just keep yuh eyes skinned!'

Benson waved and rode ahead to join Smith riding point a quarter-mile on.

'All clear?' he asked.

'Plenty of tracks t' show Whittaker and his men came this way. They were headin' f' Lateness, sure enough.'

'Still don't figure that. And why take Mrs Grey? Yuh say yuh know?'

Smith's glance was no more than a flick of his eyes. 'Mebbe.'

'But yuh ain't sayin'?'

'I'm concentratin', Sheriff. Just concentratin'.' Smith urged his mount to a gallop and pulled ahead. 'See yuh at the Canyon,' he called from a cloud of dust.

Lou sighed and pulled back closer to the stage.

Shake Reams' progress with the stage slowed through a difficult, rock-strewn stretch of the Pass as it swung to the right in the final draw to Touch Canyon. He was forced to bring the team to almost a walking pace, a fact which worried Lou Benson as he trailed alongside.

'Ain't no point in tryin' f' anythin' faster,' groaned Shake. 'Any one of these rocks could be the one that does f' us. Just have t' keep movin', and hopin'. Hold steady there!'

Benson left Shake to the driving and turned his attention to the surrounding country. The high hills had given way to the greyer, sharper sweeps of mountains. The sky above their peaks was still clear blue, but the shadows were dark and thick, waiting like open mouths to swallow whoever ventured into them.

The Canyon, with its walls of tight, sheer rock, would be darker still, but maybe that could be an advantage, thought Benson. Only trouble was, the stage was making one hell of a noise, to send echoes clattering over the rock in an eerie avalanche of sound. If there was anyone close, he would have no difficulty in knowing they were coming!

But maybe there would be no one. Maybe they were all in Lateness, and maybe they would stay there, at least for tonight...

'Canyon comin' up!' called Shake. 'Now f' the real rough goin'!'

'Yuh sure yuh can get this outfit through there?' asked Smith, reining up at the stage where it waited at the entrance to the Canyon. 'I been in there, and believe me—'

'That's my side of the business, mister!' snapped Shake. 'Just leave the drivin' t' me. Yuh keep watchin' out ahead. Yuh got it?'

'I got it,' grinned Smith.

'Good. Now let's move, shall we? Who in tarnation wants t' sit around here admirin' the view? Away there!'

It took most of the daylight hours still left to them for any progress to be made through Touch Canyon. The stage groaned and moaned its way over rocks and through the jagged cuts that riddled the ground. The team heaved, stumbled, snorted and sweated with effort, but under Shake's careful handling stayed with the task. Smith continued to wander ahead, his eyes forever scanning the rock faces for the slightest movement, but there was never more than a lone hunting hawk to attract his attention.

Lou Benson rode easy at the side of the stage, watching every protesting turn of the wheels, wincing inwardly at the creak of axles, the shudder through timbers, the tremors that threatened at any moment to wrench the outfit apart.

It somehow held together.

Just occasionally he would catch a glimpse of the pale face of Cal Heeney, the staring unblinking gaze of May Banks. Neither protested: both remained silent, deep in their separate thoughts.

The Canyon had darkened to a corridor of thickening shadows when Shake reined the team to a halt and turned to Benson.

'That's it f' now,' he sighed, wiping his face. 'Horses need t' rest up. Reckon we're a mite short of half-way through. Suggest we water the team and plan on makin' another start close on dawn.'

Benson grunted his agreement and rode on to inform Smith. An hour later the spare mounts they were trailing had been loose hitched. Shake was attending to the team and Benson and May Banks had coffee coming to the boil. Smith continued to wander, watchful and silent, close to whatever thoughts and prospects occupied him. Soon the night would gather and the Canyon and all it held disappear in the darkness.

Benson reckoned it to be well after midnight when he felt the touch of a hand on his shoulder. His eyes opened instantly and he stared into the night-shadowed face of Smith and his piercing grey eyes.

'Heeney's gone,' he whispered. 'Took one of the spare mounts. My fault. I been dozin'.'

'Hell!' mouthed Benson. 'Where's he headin'?'

'T' wherever Leonora Grey is holed up.'

'Lateness?'

'I'd reckon so.'

'But why?'

Smith grinned. 'She owes him, don't she?'

'Owes him? F' what?'

Smith's grin faded. His grey eyes

142

sparkled. 'F' killin' her husband, o'course. Or hadn't yuh figured that, Sheriff?'

Benson stiffened, then came to his feet. 'I'd figured—' he began.

'Mebbe yuh'd figured many things, and mebbe yuh were close t' understandin', but not close enough.' Smith relaxed. 'I'm goin' t' ride outta here in just one hour. And I don't have t' tell yuh where I'm headin'. But before I do that, I reckon I owe yuh somethin' of an explanation. I reckon yuh deserve t' know who killed Sam Grey and why and what those involved are plannin' t' do now—not that they're goin' t' succeed. Not if I have my way, Mister Benson...'

SEVENTEEN

Leonora Grey walked slowly, carefully round the room of the Silver Saddles hotel in Lateness and stopped when she reached the window. The street below her was empty, silent and still in the depths of the dark night. The only light was from a distant window at the far end of town, a softly shimmering glow that reminded her there were others who kept late hours and waited. But for what, she wondered?

She closed her eyes, relaxed her shoulders and let her fingers rest lightly on the fabric of her dress. It felt good to be in clean, decent clothes again—she was glad she had rigged herself out at the store that afternoon—and felt even better to have bathed and rid herself of the dust and dirt.

A pity it had all been spoiled by the man seated at the table behind her; a pity he was still alive and here, counting her money! A real shame... A situation she would have to do something about, deal with somehow...

'Quite a haul yuh got here, ma'am,' said Ord Whittaker still flicking through the pile of notes. 'Don't rate m'self much of a countin' man, but I sure know money when I see it. Sure as hell, I know money!'

'Five thousand,' snapped Leonora Grey, her stare firm on the empty street.

'That so—five thousand, eh? Well, that sure is a haul by m' standards. Five thousand... Well, now...'

She heard Whittaker shift his chair, come to his feet.

'I appreciate yuh frankness, ma'am. Nice of yuh t' fill me in on the figures.' She heard his soft giggle. 'Five thousand, plus the jewellery... Heck, I must've found m' lucky star!'

And then there was a grunt, a dangling silence she could feel in the chill at her neck.

' 'Course, that ain't all, is it, ma'am? I mean, I seen yuh take that money from the bank. I was there, right back of yuh, mostly admirin' the sling of yuh butt, I must admit, but I seen the look in that bank man's eyes clear enough. Like he might've been sayin': *Is that all, Mrs Grey? Yuh sure? There's more.* And I bet yuh gave him the nod, eh? Bet yuh set them feastin' eyes of yours right on him and shut him right up. Now ain't that so, ma'am? Shut him up just so's I f' one wouldn't know how much there is here in that goddamn bank.'

Another slower, softer step towards her.

'Am I right, Mrs Grey? Is Ord Whittaker here readin' yuh right? I reckon so!'

Leonora Grey turned delicately, graciously from the window, and smiled, her eyes sparkling. 'Of course you're right, Ord. And wrong in the same breath!' She paused, the smile shimmering, her gaze beginning to flash over Whittaker's face.

'Now listen, lady—'

'No, Mister Whittaker, you listen to me! There's plenty more money where that came from—in that same bank down the street there—and it's mine, all mine...' Her eyes flashed, her lips were suddenly softer, damper. 'How it got there ain't no business of yours.' The woman swished her skirts and turned back to the window. 'It would be very stupid, wouldn't it, to remove all that money in one go? It wouldn't look exactly decent, would it? It might look as if I was being a mite too anxious to get my hands on it so soon after my husband's death.' She turned again, this time with a smile that eased to a grin. 'You see my point, Mister Whittaker?'

'I see it clear. ma'am,' said Whittaker. 'But I also see somethin' else... I see the problem of Sheriff Benson and Jefferson Grey, and I wonder who this fella Heeney really is... And I'm gettin' fast t' thinkin' that yuh husband didn't die at the hands of no stranger. Nossir! I see yuh gettin' y'self int' a bit of a fix, ma'am—'cus the fact of the matter is, yuh gotta shift that money and clear Lateness fast. Time's runnin' out, ma'am.'

Leonora Grey's lips tightened. 'Perhaps you're beginning to see too much. But you are correct: the money has to be moved quickly. Tomorrow at the latest. And then I leave Lateness for wherever I care to spend my life, in all the comfort I so desire—with whoever I care to share it. You get me, Mister Whittaker?'

Ord Whittaker tapped the butts of his Colts. 'Oh, yes, ma'am, I get yuh clear as a frost-slicked mornin'.' His eyes narrowed. 'But how come the money's here in Lateness, and how come—'

'Never mind.' The woman's eyes were icy. 'You've got some serious thinking to do. God knows why fate threw us together—'

'I ain't complainin'!' grinned Whittaker.

'Perhaps not, but there remains the problem of the stage and what's happened at the Pass.'

'Don't worry,' said Whittaker. 'M' boys'll take care of the Sheriff and Smith. I can trust them. Good men who shoot fast and accurate. I don't figure on them havin' missed the minute their targets came int' sight.'

Leonora Grey's stare steadied. 'I wish I could share your confidence, but that's as maybe. Now, you've got to decide what to do next. You've got two choices: you can take the money on the table there, and the jewellery, and go booze and whore it till it's gone, or... Or you can stay, help me collect the rest of the cash and then come with me back East. Who knows what you may earn as a bonus!'

The woman's grin slid easily to a sensual smile.

'There ain't no choice,' said Whittaker sharply. 'I already made it. Right now!' He came quickly towards her, his hands reaching anxiously.

Leonora Grey stepped back. 'Steady! Don't let's clear the account too soon! You take yourself off for a while, go drink with your boys, and I'll see you later for whatever else this night has in store...'

The soft, thoughtful smile was still playing at Leonora Grey's lips an hour later as she continued to watch from the window. She was satisfied with her handling of Ord Whittaker. She had bought herself time. How much and how she could best use it remained to be seen, but if Cal Heeney was doing what she guessed he would, she would not have long to wait. The situation might be a deal different come sun-up; the future safe and assured.

But meantime there was still Mister Smith and the Sheriff, if either were still alive... Her smile flickered and faded, her lips were suddenly tighter, her gaze harsher. Smith, or Jefferson Grey, could

149

mean trouble. But why had he come to Steeple, and when; why had he stayed out of sight; had his arrival in the town been a coincidence; had he heard about his brother's death, or was the secrecy surrounding his visit as a result of Sam Grey sending for him? And why had he joined the stage? Did that mean...

But that was as far as Leonora Grey's thoughts went. She turned at the sound of a creak beyond the room, watched as the door opened slowly, saw the gap widen, a hand she recognised, that same hand that had moved over her flesh with such desire.

Cal Heeney stepped into the room and closed the door behind him.

EIGHTEEN

The morning was breaking clean and clear in Touch Canyon as Lou Benson and Shake Reams prepared the team for the first haul of the day.

'Just don't make no sense,' muttered Shake for the sixth time in as many minutes. 'No darned sense at all. Beats me. Who the hell is Cal Heeney, anyhow? I ain't never seen him around Steeple before. Where'd he come from? And yuh tellin' me that Mrs Grey kept him under wraps till she was good and ready f' him t' shoot her husband? She that sort of a cat-bitch? She plan the whole thing f' Sam Grey's money? Is that the size of it?'

'Reckon so,' said Benson.

'Sure, I seen Heeney goin' int' Mrs Grey's room back at High Rivers—that's what I been tryin' t' tell yuh—but hirin' him f' that is one thing, killin's another.' Shake spat. 'And where does our Mister Smith figure in all this? If Jefferson Grey—and I reckon he is, 'cus I seen that face on the Wanted posters; knew I had—if he's Sam's brother, how come he didn't step in and do somethin'? Why'd he come t' Steeple—and where in tarnation is he now?'

'Ridin' fast on Heeney's tail. Left middle of the night.'

151

'And that leaves us where?'

'It leaves us with the job of gettin' this outfit through t' Lateness. And we sure as hell will! Smith'll keep Whittaker and Heeney occupied till we get there, and by m' reckonin' we should have a clear run.'

'And there's another critter I wanna see hangin' high,' snorted Shake. 'That louse Whittaker! He did f' Big John and George Banks, not t' mention what he's done t' Mrs Banks there. Hell, Lou, we got some real settlin' t' do and no mistake!'

'Plenty,' mouthed Benson. 'So the sooner we get this stage rollin', the sooner we get t' the settlin'.'

'I'm with yuh there, Sheriff—all the way!'

Smith coaxed his mount gently through the cut of the draw and reined up. There was already the spread of a hazy morning light in the East. The country was taking shape; a distant sprawl of hills colouring under the soft glow; the flatter lands filling with a pattern of lean shadows. Somewhere beyond them, where they merged with the last of the darkness, lay Lateness.

The man's grey eyes settled in a thoughtful stare. An ordinary town, he guessed, in a nowhere special spread of the trail heading West, but soon to be an end as far as he was concerned, a final reckoning ground in the name of his brother. Sam would have wanted it that way. He had always been the one for persistence, for staying with a cause till it was done.

'Never figure a man who turns his back on a purpose...'

Smith half smiled at the memory of his brother's words. There were many things, and folk, Sam had never quite got to figuring, one of them being his wife. Sure, he had loved the woman—loved having a younger woman around him—loved her with a depth that had finally become obsessive. He had never seen any side of Leonora that was not of his own making and belief—not, that is, until close on a year back when he had been forced to admit to himself that maybe she was

153

deceiving him, that it was, after all, his wealth, and her own hands on it, she had ever really wanted.

Smith steadied his mount as it pawed at the sand and loose stone. Sam's realisation had been the beginning of his troubles, but perhaps even he had never figured on them leading to his death. Or had he? Is that why he had sent the message for his only brother to come to Steeple as soon as possible? Is that why, some four months earlier, Sam had travelled East to meet with Jefferson for the first time in years to talk to him of his doubts about Leonora, perhaps to warn him that trouble was brewing? Had he suspected then that somehow, somewhere it was all going to end in tragedy?

Smith sighed. Pity Sam had never said it right out. A pity too that it had taken Jefferson so long to reach Steeple. Maybe a day earlier would have made the difference... Maybe he, Jefferson Grey, would not be here now travelling under the name of Smith, waiting for the moment to avenge his brother's death, to see Leonora

Grey taken to account for her part in the plotting and scheming of things, and not least for her greed and deceit.

But, heck, he could well do without Ord Whittaker on the scene! Still, as Sam had put it more than once: *You're a fightin' man, Jefferson, always have been, always will be, I guess. Don't agree with it, but that's yuh way, yuh life, mebbe it'll be yuh death. And that's it, ain't it? Fightin's in yuh blood...*

So be it, thought Smith, urging the mount to a gentle gallop. Maybe there was a wry smile on Sam's face now as he watched from wherever he had gone.

Sheriff Joe Dutton was tired, troubled and getting touchy. Too many things were going wrong too fast, and that, he reckoned, was upsetting the pace of Lateness—and keeping him awake half the night!

There was the stage from Steeple for a start. Where in hell had that got to? Shake Reams was never late, so what had happened? A hold-up? And if the stage had been held up, had Ord Whittaker anything

155

to do with it? Whittaker was no sort of character to have in town, but why in tarnation had Leonora Grey ridden in with him, and why had she withdrawn so much money from the bank? What was going on?

Sheriff Dutton scratched at his stubbled cheek and paced anxiously round his office. Something was on the boil, of that he was certain. But what to do—that was his problem. He had no fancy to tangle with Whittaker and his boys, leastways not until he had something definite to tangle over. And as for Mrs Grey—well, it sure was a shame for her being widowed like that, and her still so young, but it was her money in the bank and she could handle it any way she felt fitting. Even so...

And then there was the problem of trying to fathom what Whittaker would do next. Take his fill of women and whisky and ride out, or had he some other plan building? And what about Mrs Grey; did she reckon on staying in Lateness, or had she joined up with the Whittaker gang? Ord Whittaker and Leonora Grey together? Seemed unlikely. Maybe he should go take a look, talk to Mrs Grey. Maybe he should go in search of the stage, or maybe he should stay right here in town and keep an eye on Whittaker...

'Hell!' he cursed to himself. There had never been a time in Lateness when things had been so uncertain. Never been a time when he had begun to sweat so early.

He walked quickly to the window and stared down the empty main street where the morning light was stealing in like a late hound. All was quiet. Maybe too quiet. Deep silence among shadows had a habit of shattering suddenly.

It had the feel of that sort of day coming up.

NINETEEN

The scuff of easy hooves through dust and sand, the creak of leather, jangle of tack, the snorts, the soft, lonesome whinny—these were the sounds that finally woke Lateness and brought one of Ord Whittaker's bleary-eyed sidekicks to the bat-wing doors of the Silver Saddles.

The man ran a sticky hand over his face, pushed open the doors and stepped unsteadily onto the boardwalk. He blinked, rubbed his eyes and gazed open-mouthed down the main street.

'Sonofabitch!' he croaked. 'If that ain't somethin' else...'

He moved back to the doors and called over the top of them to the gloomy interior of the saloon.

'Hey, Luke... Luke, yuh just shift yuh butt, will yuh. Come take a look at this. Luke...wake up, darn yuh.'

It was a full half-minute before Luke stumbled to the man's side and turned his own bleary gaze down the street to where a fully saddled but riderless horse made its slow, uncertain way through the morning.

'Scuttlin' snakes!' hissed Luke, wiping the backs of his hands over his eyes. 'Ain't that... Yeah, that's Cooney's horse. How come? He stayed back with the others at the stage. So how come his horse is here and Cooney ain't? Yuh reckon that sheriff and the Grey fella... Hell, if that don't take some lickin'...'

'Never mind the wonderin',' murmured his partner. 'We'd best stir Ord off that woman, I reckon...'

Smith waited and watched from the deeper shadows of a tumbledown shack close to the livery. The horse he had chosen with some care from the mounts taken at the stage shooting and turned loose the moment he hit Lateness was still moving, nearing the men at the saloon. It would take all of five minutes for the sidekicks to recognise it and decide to wake Ord Whittaker.

Five minutes would be long enough...

Smith slid from the shadows and made his way to the back of the livery. All quiet here, he thought, and moved on. He crossed quickly along the side of a corral and reached a spread of open-fronted stabling. He paused again, watched, listened. No movements, no sounds. He wondered where Heeney was holed up.

Not, he figured, at the saloon or anywhere near it. But it would have to be somewhere that gave him a clear view of the street; some place where he could keep a keen eye on Ord Whittaker and Leonora Grey.

He edged away from the stables and turned his attention to the rear of the saloon. Two doors, a flight of stairs to the first floor rooms, a narrow space between the main building and the next door store. Maybe one of the doors was open. His grey eyes narrowed in concentration, his fingers ran lightly over the butt of his Colt.

Three minutes... Four...

Whittaker would be moving by now, coming down the stairs to the saloon, cursing at having been disturbed. Four and a half minutes... An open space to the doors... Time to move.

He stepped into the strengthening sunlight, felt it warm on his back and neck, a comforting touch, and then he heard the step behind him, the whispered crunch of a boot into sand.

Smith spun round, his Colt already drawn and tight in his hand.

He saw the man through a blur, a scruffy, dark-skinned sidekick with a leering grin on his sweating face. He heard the roar of the man's gun and knew instinctively he had missed as his dive to his left pulled him clear of the sidekick's aim.

The man's grin faded to be replaced by a scowl, a glint of glazed surprise then anger in his eyes. His stare fixed on the barrel of Smith's Colt, and for a fateful second he was transfixed, his fingers no longer a part of his hands.

In the next, he was being hurled back, tossed through the air like a scrap of blown paper as Smith's first shot ripped into his chest. His feet never touched the ground in the speed and blaze of the second shot that threw him once again to leave him still and lifeless and blood-soaked on the sheen of bright sand.

Smith gave the man no more than a cursory glance as he came to his feet and bolted back to the stables.

He breathed deeply, wiped his eyes and dusted down his clothes. 'Close,' he muttered, then shot his glance anxiously to the rear of the saloon. No doubt about it now, Whittaker would be getting himself set for a stalking shoot-out.

He wondered—and smiled thinly at the thought—if Ord realised it was his long-time but fast ageing adversary, Jefferson Grey, who had just leaded one of his men to oblivion? Or would he imagine it might have been Sheriff Benson, maybe Cal Heeney... No, thought Smith, leaning back on the stable wall; no, Ord Whittaker would know right enough... Know that two shots and then silence was the mark of J.G. His smile broadened, his grey eyes sparkled.

'Your move, Ord!' he whispered, holstering his Colt smoothly. 'I'm goin' t' enjoy this!'

Smith had barely taken his next breath before one of the doors to the saloon burst open and two men, guns already blazing wild lead, fanned out across the open space to the stables.

Bullets ripped like fire sparks into the woodwork surrounding Smith. He ducked, backed and looked round hurriedly for new cover. Scant, he thought, ducking again as the men came on, but there were the broken bales of straw.

He scuttled to them, squatted as low as he could get, fumbled for a match in his pocket, struck it and watched the first lick of flame begin to spread.

One of the men had reached the stables, his gun silent, an arm raised against the gathering smoke and growing flames. Smith rose from the crackling straw like a dark drift of shadow, and with one roar of the Colt tight at his hip felled the sidekick where he stood. Smith grinned, then dodged quickly behind the smoke.

The second sidekick released a spurt of firing into the lick of flames, took a step forward, thought better of it and eased away, his Colt barrel down on a loose arm.

That was to be the man's last move, save to lift his eyes at the sight of Smith who seemed to be walking out of the flames like some shimmering demon. In the next moment the man was rolling back under the blaze of the shot that tossed him aside as if no more than a fluttering ember of the fire.

Smith slid out of reach of the flames as they licked hungrily at the stable's dry timbers. Where to now, he wondered? Back to the livery. Would he make it with half the Whittaker gang waiting for him? But if he stayed where he was he would fry...

He began to cough in the clouding smoke, moved again, this time towards the opening to the corral, but too late even as he reached the clearer air, the clean light of the sun.

Ord Whittaker faced him, tall, straight, his blue eyes steady, his lips settled in a soft smile, hands easy at his sides.

'Warm enough f' yuh, Jefferson?' he mocked.

Smith stepped back into the stable. 'Dammit!' he cursed through a splutter as the smoke reached into him again. But maybe not so surprising. Ord had always been one for the showdown; always proving himself to his boys. Never happy till he was taunting the fates...

'Always thought it might come t' this,' called Whittaker. 'Been lookin' forward t' it. Yuh still as good as ever, Jefferson, or has age slowed yuh down a mite? Mebbe yuh'd care t' show me, eh?' He laughed chillingly. 'Appreciate yuh makin' it quick, though. Don't want yuh t' cook y'self in there, and I gotta woman waitin' f' me—too hot t' leave simmerin'!'

Have it your way, Ord, thought Smith, no other is going to satisfy...

There was a sudden surge of flames, a creaking, splintering shift of timbers, a deeper groan, a rush of air and smoke. Smith saw the stable roof above him begin to sag then to lean ominously forward as the walls supporting it moaned into collapse.

Nothing else for it, he decided, and launched himself into a dust-scudding dive, his Colt fixed in his right hand.

Whittaker had backed at the rush of flames and lifted his gaze to the roof at the slow creak of its destruction—vital seconds that took his attention from the opening and Smith's only route of escape.

He realised his mistake just a half-second after Smith slid through the sand like a scorched lizard, the half-second it needed for Smith's gun to blaze in a single, roaring shot that burst clean in Whittaker's gut.

Whittaker's blue eyes brightened and widened in a dazzle as he went down, his gaze riveted on Smith's face, the ghostly drift of a smile at his lips.

'Thought I'd taught yuh better than that, Ord,' croaked Smith as he scurried clear of the flames.

TWENTY

Smith splashed cold water over him from the butt at the back of the saloon and lifted a wet, dripping face to Sheriff Joe Dutton.

'Yuh say yuh got 'em? All of 'em?' he asked, shaking his head.

'Every darned one! Locked up tight as

bugs in a blanket! They ain't goin' no place, not till the Marshal gets here.'

'What about the woman and Heeney? Where the hell are they?' frowned Smith.

'Now, yuh hold hard, mister, and steady right up there,' said Dutton, raising a restraining hand. 'Sure, I got the Whittaker mob—leastways what's left of the scum—and that don't surprise me none. Same old story, ain't it... Yuh take away the leader and the pack collapses faster than termites munchin' breakfast, and I'm appreciative of yuh efforts regardin' that... Sure was some shootin' yuh put in there... But that don't give me no good cause t' go lockin' every critter up, does it, just on yuh say-so, and it sure as hell don't tell me nothin' about a woman or a Mister Heeney or, more t' the point, who in tarnation you are!'

Dutton rested his hands on his hips. 'And then there's all this...' He nodded to the drifting clouds of smoke from the still smouldering fire at the stables. 'Darned near half m' town burned down at a cost I can't begin t' imagine...'

'That'll be taken care of,' said Smith impatiently. 'I wanna know about—'

'I know what yuh wanna know, mister, but I'm a mite more concerned with what I should be knowin'! Okay, so there is a woman here, somewhere—Mrs Leonora Grey—with a whole heap of cash, but I ain't seen nothin' or heard of no Heeney. Mrs Grey rode in with Whittaker and doubtless shared her bed with him last night. Seemed t' me t' be lookin' that way last time I cast eyes on the pair of them. That's as mebbe. I ain't got nothin' on her, savin' some pertinent questions. What I do wanna know is who the hell you are?'

'Later. Yuh can have it all later,' snapped Smith, replacing his hat. 'If yuh ain't seen Heeney, then where is Mrs Grey?'

'Heck, mister, what d' yuh take me for—a mind-reader or somethin'! How should I know? I can tell yuh she ain't in the saloon, not while I was roundin' up the Whittaker boys, anyhow. She ain't been no place in this town save the bank and the Silver Saddles, and that's a fact.'

'The bank...' mused Smith. 'There some place quiet close by it?'

'Only old Oakey's place. He died years back. Used t' run a saddlery, but the hut's been deserted these past—'

'That's it, Sheriff! Oakey's place... Mrs Grey and money are never far parted!' Smith eased his Colt from its holster and spun the chamber for a reload. 'Show me the way, Sheriff,' he added quietly.

'Hang on, mister—'

'The name's Smith.'

'Smith?'

'Yuh got it—Smith.'

'Okay, *Mister Smith,* but let me tell yuh somethin'—'

'Sheriff, we ain't got the time f' politics, law or philosophy, not in any order, not if yuh plannin' on havin' this town of yours peaceful again come sundown. Now, the stage from Steeple is rollin' close, meantime I got other business t' attend to. So yuh goin' t'show me Oakey's place or not?'

Smith tapped the barrel of the Colt in the palm of his hand.

'Sure, Mister Smith, sure I am. This way.'

'Bitch! That's what yuh are, Mrs Grey—a bitch! Yuh hear me—a bitch!'

Cal Heeney brushed aside a hanging cobweb, strode to the door of the dusty, ramshackle room, turned and glared at Leonora Grey.

'Yuh were goin' t' sell me out—*me*—f' that scum of a gunslinger, Ord Whittaker. I oughta shoot yuh now, right here, right where yuh stand!' Heeney's face gleamed with a heavy sweat. 'And mebbe I will!'

Leonora Grey stood perfectly still, her eyes hard and cold in an unblinking stare. She waited a moment, then smiled slowly, softly, until the stare was suddenly brighter and tempting.

'Cal,' she began gently, 'you aren't being very smart, are you?'

'Smart, f'crissake! Smart! Oh, I'm bein' smart, ma'am, real smart. Smarter than I been f' a long time. I should've been smart months back, then mebbe I'd have seen clear through yuh. Seen what yuh were

170

plannin' from the start.' Heeney paused and wiped the sweat from his face. 'That way I wouldn't have gotten m'self in this mess.'

He put a hand to his shoulder and winced. 'That way I wouldn't have listened t' all the sweet talk makin' up t' me, persuadin' me t' join yuh from back East, and then leavin' the final job t' me—shootin' yuh husband! F' what? The pleasures of yuh body—oh, sure, I enjoyed that, no mistake—the promise of money and you and me bein' t'gether some place. Sure, that looked good, real good, but yuh had no intention of carryin' through that part of the deal, did yuh? Yuh were goin' t' dump me and go it alone, 'ceptin' that Whittaker got in the way... But yuh weren't goin' t' let that stop yuh. Nossir! Yuh struck a deal with him, didn't yuh, and that included invitin' him int' yuh bed and leavin' me f' the night in this dirt hole! Hell! Like I say, Mrs Grey, yuh just a bitch!'

Leonora Grey had not moved a muscle or shifted her stare throughout Heeney's tirade. She had simply watched him, at times seeing through him, it seemed, to some scene in the distance, at others looking deep into his eyes. Now, as he cleared the sweat from his face again, her lips parted in a soft, sultry smile.

'You all through?' she asked. Heeney raised his eyes to her. 'All finished talking dumb? You had better be! What you're assuming is fool's talk. All right, so Whittaker was an unexpected difficulty in our plan, but I was taking care of that—in my way, a way that would have worked if that interfering Jefferson Grey hadn't shown up. Now we got real trouble.'

She paused. Heeney watched her carefully. 'Nobody saw me leave the saloon early this morning,' she went on. 'Nobody knows we're here. Lucky I found this place. But time's running out. You heard the shooting—and that means either Whittaker's killed Jefferson Grey, or Grey's settled Ord. Either way, we've got to move, and fast. I got to get the rest of the money from the bank, and then we ride. We need horses. That's your problem, but find them.' She paused again. 'You're going to have to trust me, Cal, so are you still with me or not? Make up your mind. Now!'

Heeney was silent for a moment, still watching the woman with a glazed, confused look in his eyes. 'Yuh mean—'

'I mean,' she interrupted sharply, 'that nothing's changed. We're going to leave Lateness with the money just as we planned. You're either with me or not.'

'Jefferson Grey knows, doesn't he?' said Heeney. 'He knows about us, about what we done. Yuh can see it in them grey eyes. And mebbe that sheriff knows too. Mebbe he's known all along. Mebbe we ain't been so smart as we thought...'

'Cut the doubting, Cal. This isn't the time for it. It doesn't matter now who knows or who doesn't. We are still free and the money's there—just across the street, waiting for me to pick it up. It doesn't matter a damn if Grey is here or not, or where Sheriff Benson is. We still have the time, if we move fast.'

Heeney sighed, ran a hand over his face.

'Hell—it seems like I got nothing' t' lose in stickin' with yuh.'

Leonora Grey crossed the dusty floor and placed her hands on Heeney's shoulders. 'That's my man,' she murmured through her smile. 'The good times are coming, Cal, you can be sure of that.' The smile faded. 'Give me a few minutes to get to the bank, and then move. Meet me back here in fifteen minutes. You got that?' Heeney nodded. 'Good.' She drew herself closer to him and kissed him softly on the lips. 'And no more fool talk, understand?'

A minute later, Leonora Grey had collected her valise and left the shack. Heeney watched her from the window as she strolled confidently, casually to the bank. Some woman, he thought, and maybe she had been straight with him, after all. Maybe she was...

But in the next moment his thoughts faded, his brow creased to a deep frown, his eyes narrowed, and he was sweating again.

He had seen a movement on the other

side of the street, the slide of a shape into shadow. The figure of a man—a man he knew.

Mister Smith!

TWENTY-ONE

Smith's grey eyes narrowed to dark slits as he eased back into the shadows and settled his stare on the rundown store facing him.

It looked deserted, somewhere for dust to gather and wind and rain to do their worst. Maybe—maybe not. The door to the place was tight shut, the single window black as a blind eye. Was there a backdoor, he wondered? Was Heeney in there, alone, or with the woman? Had they seen him; were they watching him?

He shifted his gaze to left and right. The street was empty. Only the door to the bank stood slightly ajar to catch the cool of the faint breeze. There were no

175

sounds, no movements, save the curl of smoke to the sky from the burned out stable.

He shrugged his shoulders, relaxed, his stare fixed again, his thoughts drifting... To the killing of Ord Whittaker, his bright blue eyes, the smile in those final moments... 'Like I said, Ord, I thought I taught yuh better,' murmured Smith to himself. 'Yuh should've known... Never break yuh concentration...'

He flinched, opened his eyes wider and re-focused his stare. He was getting old—not even listening to his own good advice! Maybe it was time to move, take a look at the rear of that one-time saddle store, see if there was a door...

The single shot from the Colt would have ripped half of Smith's face away and splattered it on the woodwork behind him had he not moved a split second before its roar from the window of the store.

'Sonofabitch!' he mouthed, stumbling back into the deepest of the shade. He waited, certain that Heeney—it could only be Heeney in there, he reckoned—would try a second shot. He saw the window close like an eye shutting in sleep, then there was only the silence and no movement.

Smith stayed motionless, conscious of the lift and fall of his breathing, the slow, cold trickle of sweat in the nape of his neck. A half-minute, a minute...long enough for Heeney to have made an escape through a back door. Another ten, twenty seconds... Time to take the gamble...

Smith moved from the shade, two, three steps closer to the street. Now his stare was tight on the store, on the spaces between it and the neighbouring buildings; waiting for the first flicker of a shadow, the slightest sound.

He halted. The morning was getting hotter, the sun higher. The heat haze shimmered across shapes, turning them to slipping, shifting blurs. He blinked, felt a line of sweat slide from his brow to his cheek, the tingle of an itch in his gun hand.

'Come on!' he murmured. 'Come on!'

The door to the store burst open like

a freak crack of lightning, with Heeney filling the space in a charging surge of limbs, his Colt blazing wildly, his face creased to a crazed, sweating grin, his eyes flashing.

Smith dived instantly and instinctively to his left, out of line of the spitting hail of lead that kicked viciously through the dirt, lost his balance and fell like a roped steer to the ground.

That might have been Heeney's moment to level his aim and have Smith at his mercy, but by now his eyes had filled with a flood of hot sweat, his shoulder wound broken in a new spurt of bleeding, and his head begun to throb with the turmoil of sound, movement, heat and the madness of fighting for his life.

He halted, legs suddenly stiff, the Colt heavy in his hand, and glared wildly round him as if expecting the street to erupt with the shimmering swirl of ghosts.

Smith scrambled to his feet, released two shots and dived again, this time scrambling for the slim cover of a broken stretch of the sidewalk. More lead from Heeney's gun, still wild, pumping fresh air and the emptiness of dirt.

Heeney wiped the sweat from his eyes and in a moment of clear vision had Smith in his sights only yards away. Smith tensed, raised his Colt, fired, saw the lead lick like a lizard at Heeney's boots, but the man did not move, barely flinched in the madness of his obsession to see Smith dead.

Heeney sneered, spat, closed his fingers tight on his gun, knowing now that one shot, one carefully measured aim, would leave Smith sprawled lifeless in a patch of blood-soaked sand.

That shot never came. Heeney turned at the call of his name.

'Cal! Cal!'

Leonora Grey stood on the sidewalk outside the bank, the valise in her right hand, her face suddenly pallid and drawn in the terror and confusion of the sight before her.

'Get back!' yelled Heeney. 'F' crissake, get back!'

The woman seemed not to hear him as she stepped into the street.

'Get back!' yelled Heeney again.

Smith had come to his feet and stood without moving, waiting for Heeney to turn to him. His grey eyes were calmer now, the stare settled, the concentration tight on Heeney's every movement.

He had a fleeting image of his brother, Sam, of how it must have been on the night of his death, standing there, talking to his wife, the shadows still and heavy in the flickering lantern light of the room at the ranch; the sudden shot, clean between the shoulder-blades, the look of dismay on Sam's face, the smile on Leonora's...

Heeney swung round. Smith's Colt roared, once, twice, opening Heeney's guts.

'F' Sam,' murmured Smith as his gun blazed again and the morning filled with the sounds of the shots and the echoes of them that spiralled on the air and were lost in the shimmer of the heat.

There were seconds, timeless and fixed, when Leonora Grey was rooted to where she stood, still clutching the valise, her gaze vague and empty on the body of

Heeney as if waiting for him to move, willing him to, frowning in disbelief when nothing happened—and then, in a flare of movement, rushing towards him.

She saw nothing of the stage as it rounded into the street; heard nothing of Smith's shouted warning, came on and was within a few feet of Heeney's body when the stage team's leading horses crashed into her.

Shake Reams yelled and heaved on the reins for a halt. Lou Benson alongside him rolled forward, grabbed for a hold, stared in horror as the woman disappeared beneath the thrashing surge of hooves.

Smith winced at the grotesque contortions of the woman's limbs, the suddenly wide-eyed look of terror on her face, the spurts of blood that filled and closed her eyes, gushed from her mouth and then, in a hideously slow flow, oozed from the mangled mess of her body.

There was a strangely suspended silence when the stage had finally groaned and creaked to a halt. The horses snorted and sweated a white mist into the morning haze, but nobody moved, and only the dollar bills from Leonora Grey's battered valise danced to the touch of the mournful breeze.

TWENTY-TWO

Sheriff Joe Dutton turned a cold, hard glare on Lou Benson and came to within a pace of him where he stood with his back to the bat-wing doors of the Silver Saddles.

'Let me get this straight, Lou,' he began, 'yuh tellin' me that Mrs Grey and that fella Heeney were in cahoots over the killin' of Sam Grey; that Mrs Grey had known Heeney years ago when she lived back East and before she married Sam; that when she tired of the marriage—that bein' part due, I guess, to the difference in their ages—she persuaded Heeney t' come t' Steeple and shoot Sam on the promise of money and, well, her favours, and f' a year or so she'd been extractin' money from Sam and stackin' it up here in Lateness? That what yuh tellin' me?'

'That's about the size of it,' said Benson. 'She'd always reckoned on inheritin' the bulk of Sam's money, but when the marriage turned sour, Sam changed his Will, cuttin' her back t' the bare bones. Even so, she managed to get her hands on a fair amount—by any means that came t' hand. She had the money transferred and deposited here all in preparation f' the day she'd be free t' spend it. It was then only a matter of gettin' rid of Sam. That's where Heeney stepped in.'

'But yuh suspected somethin' was wrong?' frowned Dutton.

Benson shrugged. 'Just a gut feelin'. I couldn't figure who'd wanna shoot Sam. Nobody in Steeple, that's f' sure. So, could it have been an outsider? I reckoned it had t' be. Sure, Mrs Grey kept Heeney well hidden—some place on the ranch, mebbe a shack well outta town. He was there perhaps four or five days, long enough t' get the feel of the ground, then... He killed Sam Grey. Trouble was, Mrs Grey made the mistake of leavin' town too soon, and travellin' too light. I decided t' follow, convinced then that she was headin' f' Lateness t' meet up with Sam's killer.' Benson paused. 'Jefferson Grey had figured otherwise.'

'Yeah,' said Dutton thoughtfully. 'Jefferson Grey... How'd he get in t' this?'

'Sam and his brother Jefferson had never been close. They lived very different lives by very different standards. But when Sam got t' reckonin' that his marriage t' Leonora was falterin', he confided in Jefferson. Guess it seemed kinda natural t' him. Later, Sam's doubts and worries about his wife deepened—mebbe he got t' wonderin' if his life was in danger, but we'll never know. Anyhow, it was then that he sent f' Jefferson—not Jefferson the brother, Jefferson Grey the gunman.

'Jefferson arrived in Steeple too late t' do anythin'. Sam was already dead. But when he boarded the stage f' Lateness with the idea of followin' Mrs Grey, he recognised Cal Heeney. He'd known

184

of him back East. Wasn't too difficult then t' begin t' put the pieces together. Mrs Grey had never really met Jefferson, leastways not close up, but somehow, f' some reason, she thought she'd seen him before, and that bothered her some. In a strange sorta way, she was lucky when Ord Whittaker came on the scene. He got her away from the threat of Jefferson Grey, or Mister Smith as he was then, but not f' long enough. How she'd have finally dealt with Ord and his boys is anybody's guess, but she'd have found a way, yuh can bet on that!'

Benson turned to the bat-wings and gazed into the bright, sunlit street. 'Ghosts...that's what they were. Ghosts... They all knew each other in a way; they'd all shared the life around Sam Grey; all travellin' t' gether, escapin' the past, but haunted by it... Just ghosts...'

'But yuh let Jefferson Grey get away,' said Dutton. 'And that's a fact, Lou. There's still a price on his head, yuh know, in spite of all that talk about him bein' retired. Retired my foot! Men

185

like him don't retire... Any idea where he might've headed?'

'None,' said Benson flatly. 'He just disappeared straight after what happened out there.' He paused. 'That sure was some mess...'

'No blame on y'self or Shake. Yuh couldn't have reined in that team, no way. If yuh ask me, Mrs Grey got what was comin' t' her, as did Heeney and Whittaker. Guess we got Jefferson Grey t' thank f' that, but that don't alter the situation none. He got away, darn it, clean outta m' town like a fadin' whisper...'

'Yeah,' murmured Benson slowly. 'He got away, like 'yuh say... I reckon that's a problem we're goin' t' have to leave t' the Marshal to fathom. Left instructions back at Steeple f' Fletch Jones t' contact him. Yuh can expect him here any time, I reckon.'

Dutton pushed his hat to the back of his head. 'Well, mebbe yuh right. Don't seem a deal I can do about it now. No, I guess m' duty lies with takin' care of things here. Get m' town back t' somethin' like normal before folk get t' expectin' shootin's everyday! Yuh headin' f' Steeple?'

'He sure is!' said Shake Reams, pushing open the bat-wings. 'Just as soon as yuh ready, Lou. Stage is all set t' roll.'

'What about Mrs Banks? How's she feelin'?'

Shake sighed and scratched his chin. 'Rotten right through, if yuh ask me. Darn shame... Wicked shame... But I figure she'll be better when we get her t' Steeple. There's folk there'll take care of her. Ain't nobody goin' t' see her life blow away like dust. Nossir!'

'See yuh again, then, Lou,' smiled Dutton.

'Not so soon,' grinned Benson. 'I ain't plannin' on doin' much travellin' f' a while. Lookin' f' a quiet life.'

'Quiet life! As a sheriff? That's one helluva hope, mister!'

Two miles out of Lateness on the trail heading eastwards for the town of Steeple, with the sun high and hot in a cloudless sky, Shake Reams eased the stage team to their own pace and cast a quick glance at the man perched alongside him.

'High Rivers come sundown,' he called above the beat of hooves, the creak of leather and rolling timber. 'Guess they'll have cleared up there by now. Shan't be sorry t' see the place again, spite of everythin'. No, shan't be sorry... Still, got the stage through after all that. Ain't never failed t' get a stage through yet.'

Sheriff Lou Benson grunted and tipped the brim of his hat against the sun's glare.

'Some journey,' said Shake. 'Sure wouldn't wanna make a habit of runs like that! Nossir! Still, I guess yuh done right by Sam Grey, and the territory'll be a sight healthier without the likes of Ord Whittaker foulin' it up. And that's a fact! Some critter!' He spat into the sand. 'But who'd have thought Mrs Grey'd turn out like that? Who'd have thought it, eh? And her a real classy lady. Don't make no sense, 'ceptin' t' prove that yuh can just never tell. Why'd she wanna go and do a thing like that, with a fella like Heeney, when that husband of hers would've given her anythin'? All she had t' do was ask.'

'Askin' gets a mite greedy on occasions,' grunted Benson.

'Yeah,' said Shake. 'Greed... Anyhow, who d' yuh reckon gets Sam's money now?'

Benson shrugged. 'Mebbe Jefferson Grey is his only livin' relative.'

'Could be at that.' Shake spat again. 'Can't fathom him disappearin' like he did. Must've reckoned yuh really would've taken him in.' He glanced hurriedly at Benson. 'Would yuh?'

But Sheriff Benson did not answer. He simply adjusted his hat and fixed his gaze on the blue of the far horizon.

'Well,' mused Shake, 'mebbe yuh would, mebbe yuh wouldn't.' He leaned forward and peered into the dusty haze of the trail ahead. 'And mebbe yuh goin' t' get the chance t' decide! Look who's up ahead.'

Benson sat stiffly upright and stared at the man standing at the side of the trail a quarter-mile ahead. 'Well, now,' he murmured, 'ain't that a sight f' sore eyes!

Rein up, Shake. I got a feelin' the fella's lookin' f' a ride.'

Smith's grey eyes sparkled as he watched the stage grind to a halt.

'Thanks,' he smiled, looking up at Benson and Shake. 'Thought I might catch yuh hereabouts.'

'Lost yuh horse?' asked Benson.

'Sent him packin' back t' Lateness. Weren't mine in the first place. I been many things, Sheriff, but I ain't never got t' horse thievin'. T'ain't in m' line.'

'And now?' frowned Benson. 'Where yuh headin'? Steeple?'

'Seems like a good idea. Can't reckon on a better notion. Yuh got Mrs Banks aboard?'

'Right there in the coach,' said Shake.

'Good,' said Smith. 'I'd like a word with her. Thought I might be able to help with fixin' up her future. Seems like the least I can do.'

'I'd figured yuh might,' said Benson. 'Okay, take a seat. Next stop High Rivers.'

'I'm obliged t'yuh, Sheriff. We'll talk later.'

190

'Anytime,' said Benson.

'Heck, Lou,' said Shake when the stage was rolling again, 'what yuh goin' t' do now? He's walked right back int' yuh hands! Yuh got him! Clean as a whistle!'

'Who?' asked Benson.

'Jefferson Grey, o'course.'

'I ain't seen him.'

'Ar, come on now, Lou! We just picked him up!'

'Yuh seein' ghosts or somethin'?' grinned Benson. 'We just picked up Mister Smith. Remember? Mister Smith...'

'Yuh mean t' say—'

Keep 'em rollin', Shake! Just keep 'em rollin'...'

This Large Print Book for the Partially sighted, who cannot read normal print, is published under the auspices of

THE ULVERSCROFT FOUNDATION